Darkest Deeds in Deepest Dorset

Alethea Lawson

Published by Annwyn House in 2019
Derby, UK
annwynhouse.weebly.com

This is a work of fiction. Names, characters, places and incidents are either the product of the author's imagination or are used fictitiously, and any resemblance to actual persons, living or dead, or to actual events, is entirely coincidental.

Cover illustrations by Nell
Cover design by Angela House

Contents

Alethea Lawson

PREFACE

The author's childhood, and the setting for this novel

The manuscript of this novel was written by our Mother, but was never published. It has lain undisturbed and forgotten in our attic for the best part of 20 years, and only came to light again when we were having a clear-out, in preparation for moving to a new house. I (Anthony) dictated this novel onto my computer, and am most grateful to my two sisters, Diana Armitage and Daphne MacKerrell, and my daughter Sarah, who have kindly proof-read, and corrected, the text.

Our Mother was born in Concordia, Argentina, where her father was an Anglican Minister in the South American Missionary Society (SAMS). At the age of six or seven, she and her family came back to England, and she grew up in Dorset.

Our Mother told us that she was writing a novel, centred on the village of Tollard Royal on the Dorset/Wiltshire border, where she grew up. Although the plot and characters in this novel, came entirely from our Mother's fertile imagination, we believe that the setting of the novel, in Larmer Magna village in Dorset, is based on the village of Tollard Royal. She had a very happy childhood in this village, seeing lambs being born in springtime, feeding hens and collecting eggs from the henhouse, and apples from the orchards in autumn, and going carol singing all around the village and at outlying farms before Christmas. As a child, Mother used to love to go and collect the freshly baked bread from the bakery in the village. She loved to eat the bread warm, straight from the oven, which was delicious. Mother had a pet duck called Dilly, which she told us, used to follow her everywhere.

In the 1940s, when we were taken to Tollard Royal by our Mother, water for drinking and cooking in the Rectory (where she had been brought up) was drawn from the well below the tennis court in the garden of the rectory, near to the drive gate where it opens onto the village street. There was a glass carafe of drinking water in the bathroom, with an upturned drinking glass on top of it, for cleaning our teeth. I can remember that when the bath taps were turned on, the bath water coming out had a definite brownish tinge to it. This was because water for washing, was collected in a large cistern higher up the valley, which was fed by a series of Y-shaped field drains.

We believe that "the well at Beech Farm," which appears at the start of this novel, is based on the well in the garden of the Tollard Royal Rectory. The rest of the novel follows from there. The Rectory was thought to have originally been a farmhouse, probably dating from the reign of Queen Anne.

The other place which appears in this novel, is the fishing village of Coverack, on the Lizard Peninsula in Cornwall. It was here, that Mother had many happy holidays as a child, and later took us, her own children and our family, there. We had marvellous days there, walking over the cliff tops, swimming, playing in the sand, and going mackerel fishing.

We believe that all the characters in this novel are fictitious, with one exception. This exception is the character of the Rev Canon Pendleton, which we believe is based on the character of our Mother's father, our Grandpa, who was a much-loved Rector of Tollard Royal for about 30 years. He had twinkling eyes, and a beaming smile. Our Mother was devoted to him, as was everybody. He kept some pedigree stock: saddleback pigs, Indian Runner ducks, and white Wyandot hens, in nearby fields. Grandpa fertilised and cross-bred daffodils which he used to show, and won several prizes.

Every year our Grandpa held an out-door Memorial Service for the souls of the Quakers, in a remote valley in the Dorset Downs, some miles from Tollard Royal. Quakers used to live here 200 years ago and are buried in this valley. Some of the people who lived in Tollard Royal, thought that they had seen an apparition in the garden of the Rectory, a lady of small stature, wearing 18th century clothes, a grey bonnet and shawl and a long dress, which they called "The Little Grey Lady". Our Grandpa thought he had seen this "Little Grey Lady", who seemed friendly and happy, and was perhaps the soul of a lady who had lived here long ago, and loved this garden as much as he did. But our Mother never saw this apparition.

Other books written by our Mother include:

Freedom from Stress, about relaxation techniques that she taught to expectant mothers in ante-natal clinics, and to other patients with stress-related problems.

On a Sea of Time, a book of poetry that she wrote after her retirement, which won a Midland's Poetry prize.

This book is dedicated to the memory of our Mother, and the happy time she had as a child, growing up in Tollard Royal.

Anthony Henry, Diana Armitage and Daphne MacKerrell
2018

1. <u>The mysterious finding in the well at Beech Farm</u>

"Aye! Lots of queer things 'ave 'appened in that tharr 'ouse — it be so old. It be no wonder folk tell them tales about Beech Farm," said Bill, in the rich brogue of this Dorset/Wiltshire country, as he shook his head knowingly at the grey farmhouse. It looked as if it grew out of the soil of the rambling garden surrounding it, nestling amongst huge trees, part of the landscape of the narrow chalk valley that lay between blunt slumbering humps of downs.

"What tales, Bill?" Kate Fletcher asked nervously.

"All sorrts," Bill said. "They figure it was a hideout for them Quakers on the run from the soldiers. The Little Grey Lady could tell a story or two if she could speak".

"But who is she? If she could speak?"

Bill gave Kate a quick sideways glance. "I'll have the boss on to I if he catches I standing talking like this, see", and he hurried away down the drive to join his mate digging a trench for the sewer these new owners, the Fletchers, were having put in. They were joining Beech Farm to the main drainage which reached the village four years ago.

Suddenly, Kate felt uneasy as she looked at the old house. The Little Grey Lady! What did he mean? Kate looked at the steep downland slopes on either side of the garden at the house. All that remained of the farm now was its name, and some outbuildings. Doubts and fears surged through her. She could feel the hair beginning to bristle on her neck. She gave herself a mental shake: how stupid can you get, letting yourself get nervous like this, for no reason at all — no logical reason!

She went indoors to start clearing up some of the mess left by the plumbers and joiners who had finished work at last. While she worked, she was remembering the impact this place had made on her the moment she walked into it: she could smell the oldness - it was the musk drawn from centuries of the slow curing of a house. Time had polished its floors.

She wondered who had trodden the creaks into the oak staircase. How many hands had held the banisters before her own? Who had died in these bedrooms? Who had shivered in the draughts before David had put in the central heating? As they sat at the table, who sat with them? How many children had been comforted here? She would walk past the half open doors almost expecting to hear the murmur of voices - but she heard none. Who had whispered in the night – who stood in the hall and at the foot of the stairs? As she stared out of the windows she thought how they had all looked out of these windows onto this same garden. They had walked down the passage and heard the wind rattle the door latches. David wound the clock which told the same hours which chimed for them - do they still hear it? These walls and ceilings were the same size that they had been - it was the same space filled with their voices, but she heard no sound. She raised her eyes and knew the room was crowded, but saw nobody.

She gave a sudden shiver and shook her shoulders. Would it have been better if they have never come here? None of it made sense, but in some strange way this house was dominating her life these days. They didn't have to buy it. She and David could have gone on living in the apartment in Salisbury quite happily. Then she remembered how excited David had been when they moved in a month ago, especially when he discovered the cellar had a blocked up Tudor window. Even some of the old leading from the lattice panes were still there. Though the present house was Queen Anne, the original farmhouse must have been Tudor.

She put up the step ladder and started pasting paint stripper on the old ceiling beams in the hall. It was better to keep her hands busy... anyway there was a lot to be done, as she and David were doing all the interior decorating themselves. She looked round the square roomy hall with its low ceiling. This was the oldest part of the house, probably the original farmhouse kitchen, David thought. It felt lived in too, had an enduring feel, yet these walls spoke of sadness. Someone had cried here, quite a lot.

But why did this house seem to fold them both to itself, from the moment they saw it? In spite of being a stranger to this country scene, it had made her feel that this was the place to put down their roots, start and rear their own children. She had even privately planned to come off the pill, when they had completed the interior decorating, and next spring's gardening.

They had been married two years now. Before that she had travelled the world doing secretarial work— to experience the fullness of life, she had mistakenly thought. After three years of this she had returned to the London she knew, but found now she was a stranger to it. She could no longer accept the old round of parties and conventions, she felt nervous of it all. As there was no one there who could share her own experiences, she felt out of it, and a misfit wherever she went. Yet to go away again was running away, and she had no special place of her own to run to. Her main comfort in London was its anonymity. She could hide in that, even though it was a loneliness. Then quite accidentally she met David. For her he was a happiness she had not believed existed. Shortly after this they married. When they had found Beech Farm, she knew that this was at last her home.

She worked fast and excitedly, as gradually the black oak of the rough solid beams reappeared from under the paint. But all the time she was working the question: "Who is the Little Grey Lady?" kept threading through her thoughts, until she could think of nothing else. Little Grey Lady!

She stopped work suddenly. Before going on any further she'd got to go down the drive to where the men were digging the sewer trench, and get a categorical answer out of Bill, else there was no peace for her. When she reached the two men, they were so engrossed in peering down a deep hole, that they never heard her approach.

Bill was saying to Ernie, his mate, "Nay! That b'ain't sacking that b'ain't! That be clothing, an' women's clothing. That's a fact, it be."

"Jeese! You be roight, Bill," Ernie said in a voice grow hoarse with horror.

"That be a dead body, Ernie, that be," said Bill with conviction.

Kate jumped down into the trench beside them, and both men looked up with a start.

"What's happened? What is it?" her voice was shrill with alarm.

"We come across this well see, while we be digging this sewer. we pulled its walls down level with this trench, sliced across the wall in a manner of speaking," Bill began, looking both embarrassed and frightened at the same time.

"Yes, yes, I know. The former owners got all their drinking water from it. They told us about the well. What have you seen down it?"

"Looks like a body, Ma'am."

"Oh God, No!"

"Looks like it. Best see for yourself. Steady now! Hold on to Ernie and I, while you take a good look down it."

"It be my guess it be down tharr some time," said Ernie.

Kate could see the black glint of water, and wedged across it was a bundle of clothing in the shape of a human figure. She thought she could see the toe of a shoe propped against the well side above the water line. The stench rising from the black glassy depths was indescribable.

She turned away and sank against the trench walls, and heaved into the chalky soil. She couldn't stop the shaking of her jellied limbs, and yet they felt clamped in ice. The chestnut tree, the drive gate, and the two men, slid round in a spinning spiral, with the well at its vortex. Then she could just hear Bill's voice in the distance saying: "Nip up to the house, Ernie, and you to get a drink of water for 'er. Quick as yer can boy! See if yer can find a brandy or whisky in any of them cupboards, and bring it down 'ere. Quick lad!" Then she felt Bill pushing her head down between her knees.

After a while she could quite clearly see the sharp edges of the flint stones, and the white clods of caked chalk soil in the bottom of the trench under her. They kept quite still and solid. She raised her head and saw Bill's strained face above her.

"I'm all right now. I'm sorry to do that on you. It hit me without warning."

"Of courrse, Of courrse!" Bill might have been soothing an injured sheep dog. "Ah! 'Ere's Ernie with a drink for yer. Good lad, 'e's brought a drop o' scotch with it."

They lifted her out of the trench, then they all three sat on the bank at the side of the drive. Then Bill's breathing caught her attention - a series of hissing gasps, his face had suddenly gone as pale as chalky soil caking his boots.

"Take a swig of this, Bill", Kate said as she handed him the whisky bottle. "Ernie, would you go up to the house and put the kettle on for some tea for all of us?" She felt in possession of herself again, even if not of the situation.

When Bill's colour had returned, she asked "what do we do now?"

"We do nothing till we finish this tea, see. We'll all feel better then. After that I'll go down on my bike and see if Bob Cope's tharr, 'e be the constable round these parts. But 'e may be out, I know 'e be 'aving trouble with poachers up Chettle way. Ye'd best telephone Mr Fletcher while I be gone. I'll come straight back after I've been down to Bob's."

*   *   *   *   *

She rang David at the firm of architects where he was a junior partner, but he was out viewing a site. She left a message for him to ring her as soon as they could get hold of him. Yes, it was an emergency — a body had been found down their garden well. Yes, she did feel a bit panicky. Yes, they were looking for the local Bobby. She was keeping cool, but ask David to hurry.

She sat in the hall, on the bottom rung of the ladder, and tried to think calmly.

If only they had never come here at all. If only they had bought one of the other houses they had looked at, instead. She stared round at those silent walls as they closed in on her. Her eyes were vivid blue with accusation.

"You knew all the time! Why didn't you warn me?" she demanded out loud.

2. An Inspector calls

When David got home two hours later, he was astonished to see Kate up the ladder, frantically peeling off paint with a stripper, as if time was running out.

"You poor love! What a ghastly thing to happen to you. I wish I'd been here, how do you feel, still a bit ropey darling?" he said.

"Yes."

"It's such a rotten shock — it's the shock of it..."

"Yes," she cut him short.

"Couldn't you stop all that and come down the steps? Let's sit together and have a cup of coffee or something, while we get used to it all."

"No."

"Oh, come on Kate. There is not all that urgency about those beams. Give yourself a chance, darling. You need to rest after a shock like that."

"Can't you see... I can't handle this... this thing... in any other way?"

He heard the desperation in her voice, and saw that pretty face with its slow gentle smile, taut and grim with fierce anger, almost as if she were protecting something. He let it ride the way she wanted it.

He sat on the bottom rung of the steps. "When you told me on the phone, that the workmen couldn't find the local Bobby, I rang the Salisbury police from the office and told them about it. They'll be here in droves, any moment now, I guess."

She never took her eyes off the beam over her head. "What will happen to that — thing — in the well? They'll have to lift it out, won't they?" She was pushing hard at the old pasted paint, peeling it off in long coils. It was flaking onto his own hair and city suit — but none of that mattered to him right now.

"Oh yes, but that's their job. No need for us to be around while that's going on."

"I wonder how long it's been there?"

"The pathologist will tell us that."

"What'll they do with... it?" asked Kate.

"Put it in a mortuary I suppose, while the pathologist gets busy on it. They'll have a look for traces of identification. If they find any, they'll have to issue a description for anyone to come forward, I imagine."

"Is it a woman?"

"They rather think it is, they could see the clothing. Half the village seems to be standing around at the end of our drive. News travels fast here." His voice took on an artificial cheerfulness. "I should think business will be pretty brisk in the King John's Arms tonight."

Kate kept silent. It seemed as if the house ached with silence.

David went on in the same forced cheerfulness; "I think I will make a start on this wall opposite, this weekend. I'm convinced when I get all their plaster and some of the brick down, we'll find it's blocking up an original open fire place. I've tapped it all round, and measured up, and the whole thing fits. I'll bet it was the old fireplace when this hall was the farmhouse kitchen. It's exciting, isn't it! I'll start on it on Saturday."

If he was hoping to divert her attention into the thrill of further discovery of their home, he had failed. It seemed as if she had not even heard him. She just murmured "a woman... that makes it worse".

He had had enough. She mustn't to this. "For God's Kate, do stop that! And you're jabbing at those beams so hard, you'll be hacking chunks off the priceless oak underneath. I wish you'd come down. I could use a bit of comfort myself."

She put down the scraper, and climbed down the ladder. She stood beside him and flicked the paint peelings off his hair and shoulders. He stood up to take her in his arms.

"No David, don't do that. It'll undermine me, and the house wouldn't like that. People who live here mustn't weaken. They don't let things like life and death upset them... it's gone on here for too long."

He laughed and felt better. "I see. We've got a new Kate at the house's bidding, have we? Well perhaps the house wouldn't object to her making her husband a cup of coffee."

Her voice was her own again as she said, "after that, let's get out of this wretched house. I hate it now." He looked at her quickly and anxiously. "Let's go for a walk David, away from the direction of the well and the drive. Let's walk up the Downs."

He laughed, relieved. "That's the girl I know," and she let him put his arm around her, as they went along to the kitchen.

*   *   *   *   *

When they got back from their walk, the drive was full of police cars and blue uniforms.

A man in a grey suit and Macintosh was waiting by the front door. He was a thin wiry looking type. He approached David.

"I'm Detective Inspector Williams, Sir. May I come in for a few moments to ask you for some details about this case?"

"Certainly. We'd better go into the sitting room, it's the only room that's straight so far. We are still in a mess from alterations and workmen. You won't need to question my wife, I take it?" She had taken enough pasting from this shock. It was that tight grip that bothered him, if only she'd cry and get it off her chest, the way she usually did. Damn the influence of this house!

"Not for the present, anyway."

Inspector Williams sank into an armchair. He looked round the pleasant room. The afternoon sun slanted through the windows in gold dust bars. Bright blue brocade curtains swelled gently in the light puffs of a breeze. Tortoise-shell butterflies were feathering on a buddleia at the side of the lawn.

"It's beautiful here, Mr Fletcher, if you'll excuse me saying so," Williams said, serenity beginning to smooth out the pleats round his eyes and mouth. He had one of those anxious, alert, pale faces, with grey eyes that appeared convincingly vague at the moment. It added up to an image very different from that of the brilliant detective.

David looked at him. Strange how this house touched everyone who entered it. At this moment, the crime squad detective looked like anybody's husband.

"Yes, we love it. By the time we've finished with it, it'll be really beautiful. So you can imagine what a shock this has been to us, especially to my wife, she saw the body down the well. I wonder if you could leave her out of your enquiries as much as you can, refer them all to me, either at my office in Salisbury, or here. If you needed me here, it takes about half an hour to get back from Salisbury."

"I'll do what I can over that. It must have been a horrible experience for your wife, quite apart from the fact that it's not funny to have this pushed on you, when you're a young couple starting life in a new home."

So, breathalysers apart, the Force was human! He called through the door, "Kate darling, make us some tea, there's a love."

He sat down opposite the inspector. "I'm afraid we can't help you much, as we are so new here ourselves. We don't know anything about the village yet, haven't had time. We've done nothing but work on this house ever since we moved in."

"And how long ago was that?"

"Exactly a month ago. We moved in, in the middle of July."

"When did you buy the property?"

"On April the 15th. Then we got the plumbing ripped out, and the house joined up onto the mains supply which was already in the village. We had central heating put in, and a few structural alterations, before we moved in ourselves. At the moment, as you can see, we're joining the drains to the main drainage system in the village."

Williams noted the points in his book. The grey eyes had lost their vagueness — he looked less like anybody's husband now. "Did you know about the well?" he asked crisply.

"Yes, vaguely. We bought the property off Miss Marion Ferguson. We told her we were going to have the mains water supply put in, and asked her how she and her father had managed to get on without it. She told us that they drew their drinking water from a well beside the drive, near the gate. The domestic supply was pumped up from a rainwater tank sunk in the ground, near the house. Amazing how people can still live like that in this day and age."

"It's all a matter of what you're used to. The property belonged to Colonel Ferguson before he died, I believe."

"Yes, the lady's father. He died about two years ago."

"When did Miss Ferguson leave Beech Farm?"

"Oh, ages ago. A few weeks after her father's death. She told us she tried living here alone at first, but found it too lonely. So she went to live in Salisbury, where she had a teaching job at that time."

"Is she still there?" asked Inspector Williams.

"No. she moved shortly afterwards to take a job in the North... Nottingham I believe."

"Would you have her address?"

"You can get it from her Salisbury solicitors, Carter and Browne."

"Yes, thank you. She must have been in Nottingham a little under two years?"

"I think so," said David.

"We can check on all that. Would you know if she ever returned to the property after she left it, that's to say before you bought it?"

"I should very much doubt it. We bought all the furniture she left behind here, it was all protected under dust covers. They are wonderful antiques, the sort of stuff you don't often see. Some of these Chippendales are really show pieces. And every period fitted in so well here, in every way, we bought the lot".

"But she never returned here herself?"

"I don't believe she could have brought herself to do so. We only met her once, in April on the settlement day. She seemed very upset, especially when she spoke of the place, in a tight, closed in sort of way. You see, she'd lived here all her life, and loved all of it very greatly. It was tragic for her when her father died, and she found she just couldn't live here alone. She spoke of this house as if it was a part of herself. I think she was a very sensitive sort of person, and certainly under great stress when we met. I've a pretty good idea she'd go anywhere on earth, rather than have to renew the pain of having to say goodbye to all this again. I may be quite wrong, but that's certainly the impression I got."

"How old would you say she is?" asked the Inspector.

"Hard to say, she was quite upset at the time, I think she'd been crying. But I'd think at a guess, about mid-20s. She did smile once, and then her whole face lit up, and she looked a lot younger than that."

"You noticed a lot about her in that one meeting. You liked her?"

"Yes, immediately. She must have really loved this place. You see, she let me buy all these valuable antiques for a song. If she'd flogged them to the dealers, she'd have got three times what I paid for them. I wrote to her about it, thought it'd only fair to point this out. But she wrote back saying that she was aware of that, only it was more important to her to let the furniture stay on in the house, still a part of it, otherwise the house would miss it. She wanted to feel it was here being cared for by people who valued it, the house would like that. And now the house has got Kate, my wife, doing it too."

"Doing what?" asked the Inspector.

"Talking about this house as if it was human. No inspector, I know she could never have come back having made such a hellish break with it. We really felt very sorry for her. I know what we feel about this place ourselves, and we've only lived here a month. Imagine what it must be like for the poor girl, after 20 odd years."

"And that's all she told you about the well?"

"Yes. She did say that she was glad we were going on to the mains, as the well would have been in disuse since she left, about two years. So it would probably not be healthy, all gummed up with muck and stuff."

"Did she locate it for you?"

"She said it was under the big chestnut tree, beside the drive, and near the gate; to watch out for it as the sides were not raised like most wells, it was level with the ground. She said it had wooden shutter doors across it. But before leaving, she had laid a piece of corrugated iron over the top, as a safety measure, in case the well doors had rotted under all leaves down there."

"Did she describe how they wound the buckets up from the well?"

"Oh yes, she did. She said there was once a winch with a wire cable, but the uprights holding it might have rotted off by now. But whatever had rotted it was all quite safe, because of the protection of the corrugated iron sheet she'd put over the top of everything. She was too upset for us to ask too many questions — it wasn't fair — you could see the struggle."

"And did you ever look for the well when you moved in?"

"No. We had every intention of doing so at some time, but there's been such an enormous amount to do. As we weren't going to use it, it wasn't important, so we just put it off until we had more time, I suppose. In fact, we'd never really thought about it."

"She was dead right about the leaves. My men found the wire cable and rotting parts of the fallen winch among them."

"And the corrugated iron on top of the well?"

"No. The whole top and the well walls had been dismantled already by the men working on the sewer. But of course they'll be interviewed, and the picture of the well top as seen by them, will have to be reconstructed."

"Ah, here's the tea. Darling, I've been telling Inspector Williams about that nice Marion Ferguson, and our bargain in antiques."

Kate said quietly "yes, she was nice — but pathetic too. She seemed lost... as if the bottom had dropped out of her world. I hope she can manage her life outside this village on her own."

"I'd think she could as she's mid-twenties, Mrs Fletcher," said the Inspector.

"I don't think age has anything to do with it. She looked a frightened sort of person. She needs looking after. I often have her on my mind, as I'm working round the house. So if you have to interview her, the way you've done with David, would you remember that?"

Detective Inspector Williams said gently, "I'll remember, Mrs Fletcher." There was more to this lass than just the pretty girl that she looked.

3. **An evening stroll and the Summerhouse**

They both felt restless that evening. They found themselves scraping away at old paint on old beams in silence, in the warm twilight after a golden summer's day.

David looked across at Kate. He could see the droop of her face and her shoulders. He suddenly stopped work.

"Come on darling, let's go out for a bit of a walk."

They walked up through the garden in the opposite direction from the drive and the village, to that part where it straggled off into a beech copse. There was a wide clearing in the middle of the copse where the former owners had built a summer house. They sat on the grass in front of it, and watched the luminous sky. The air was sweet with the smell of earth, and dew soaked grass. Sleepy birds were fidgeting, and settling in its perfume.

David was smiling at her, and took her hand.

"Kate, we're going to have to face quite a deal of grimness round our precious home. But when we get right down to the nitty-gritty, we've got all of this. So we'll escape out here, and use it, and then it won't get too bad. It'll only be for a few months, then it'll all be over, and we can get on with our lives."

She didn't answer. She had her head turned slightly away, but he could see her soft full mouth, creased taut and thin.

"It's true you know, darling," he went on in a coaxing voice.

"No. For me it isn't."

"You'll find it will be. This is just the initial shock."

"David, couldn't we... sell up and go?"

"Oh look! You must not get all this out of proportion. You can't seriously mean leave Beech Farm?"

"I do. I want to leave it to its ghosts. It has let me down. I don't want any part of it now," there was such a bitterness in her voice.

"Now listen!" She turned her round to look at him. He said firmly, "it's not Beech Farm that's let you down, it's human nature. This house is not a person, it's a pile of stone, bricks, timber and mortar, a beautiful ancient pile, but that's all. Whoever the human being is, you and I don't even know... they are nothing to do with us. As for ghosts, that is sheer nonsense. The building material that makes Beech Farm could just as easily be pulled down, so that the place didn't exist, it is only building material. So do get that into your head, instead of this crazy sort of nonsense."

Then suddenly she was in his arms, crying like a winter waterfall in spate. He held her very closely. All he could do was to rest his cheek against her forehead and murmur, "that's the girl, just let it rip."

Later, when she was calmer, he talked to her gently. "The whole story behind this, whatever it was, is only part of your actual — atmosphere — bit. After all, human nature in all its forms, including birth and death, has worked itself out here for centuries. This death is just another something on the scene. It'll pass just as everything else has, and our lives will go on, until we too become part of its history. And that's how we must think of it."

"Yes, but... murder... or perhaps suicide!".

"Or even an accident, how do we know? But even so, what is that? Everything could have happened here, and probably did. The Quakers perhaps hid in these very beech trees round us, until the soldiers had gone. So this moment is just another point in time, around the fabric of our house. When you buy an old house, you buy its history too. So, think of it that way darling."

"I was trying to when you got back from Salisbury. It's difficult, this is not history. And what will we do now about the baby in the spring?"

"What baby?"

"Oh, I meant to tell you. I've got it all worked out. We'll have the inside work finished by March. Then I could stop using the pill, and while my inside was settling down in April, we could get all the spring gardening done. Then we'll be all set to start my pregnancy in May."

He shouted with laughter. "We would. Anyhow it's nice to be warned when I'm expecting to start the father-bit."

"But it was a good idea, David, wasn't it?"

"Not very. We'll do all that in time, but not yet. I'd much rather just be *us* for a while yet, selfish brute am I?" He kissed the tip of her nose. "We need time to slot in here first, get the feel of this different life for us. I'll try out that motor mower Dad gave us this weekend. We've got so much to learn about gardening, and all sorts of things, before we start rearing babies. It's going to be fun, and we've got bags of time." He dried her cheeks.

"But the house would like..."

He interrupted her. "Remember, the house is just a pile of building material. We are its owners, and we bought it with cash, so we are its boss, and can do just as we like with it."

They sat on, and watched in the gentle evening air. The peace and the hush did its work. Later, David said "it's getting chilly. Let's sit inside the summer house, it'll be warmer there. We can see the evening from it just the same. Do you know, we've never been inside it yet."

The door into it looked old and rickety, but to their surprise it opened easily, almost as if it was of oiled hinges.

"David, just look! We'd no idea — just look at this".

"Mmmm. Cane table and chairs, crockery, even a camp cooker and a kettle. God, there's even a coffee percolator! And look, it's got some old gummed-up coffee in it."

"And these tins... tea in this one... biscuits in this. The lot! What's in the corner, David?"

"Cushions, looks like. Let's see."

There were certainly cushions, but underneath them were some rugs and a folded roller bed. They stared at each other in the darkness, wide eyed with alarm and suspicion.

"Looks like someone's been living here," David said at last. He snapped open his lighter, and walked round peering through the dim rim of light.

"It's all pretty dusty. It obviously hasn't been used just recently."

"But who could it be? Why here? You can only reach it by going through the garden and passing by the house," Kate whispered.

"Let's not be too sure. What happens at the far end of this spinney?"

"It's light enough by this moon to see, let's walk through the trees and find out."

They found a path behind the summerhouse.

"Mind you, there's probably always been a path here, we mustn't allow imagination to run away with us." David was emphasising it in that down-to-earth tone he used on a site.

"But why? A path to where?"

"We'll soon find out."

The path curled in and out of the trees, up a bank and then down a bank, until it reached a hedge on the far side. There was a break in the hedge, as if made by a constant pushing through it. They pushed through it themselves on to a narrow lane no wider than a field gate. Its flint and chalk soil track between tangled hedgerows glimmered strangely white in the moonlight.

"We'll walk along it this way in the direction of the main road, see where it comes out," said David, and took her arm.

A mile further on the lane imperceptibly threaded into the main road, its junction almost hidden by high banks and hedges. This was the main road that ran up from the village, then climbed up the hill over the downs, finally dropping down to Shaftesbury, 8 miles away on the other side.

They turned right, and walked down the hill in the direction of the village. Their own house would be the first building they would come to. After a while, they could see it nestling below, among its trees. An apricot moon inked shadows around it. How still it looked, as if waiting for them. They turned into their drive gate, and still in total silence, with averted heads, walked past the well and sewer trenches, past the great mounds of thrown up soil that loomed ghostly grey-white. That chalk had buried too many secrets.

They stopped for a moment outside the house. The moon silvered the ancient roofs and walls; she rode above them, ineffably lovely, gracious, regal. Stars were like cinders in the sky. The whole silver landscape seemed to hold its breath. They could feel the silence. David broke it with "that moon looks as round as an aspirin. I suppose we ought to tell the police about what we've seen tonight."

*   *   *   *   *

By the next morning Kate was more like her usual cheerful self. All the same, before he left David suggested "why don't you drive into Salisbury in the Mini later, and join me for lunch? It'll get you away from all this police thing for a bit, they're bound to be swarming round today."

"I'll do that. But David, don't let's tell them about the summerhouse yet. When you get back this evening, let's walk the other way up that lane, and see for ourselves where it goes to. I'm dying to know now."

"Okay, Detective Inspector Kate, we will. See you..."

He was smiling as he drove off. At least now she was caught up in that feminine curiosity, rather than emotional involvement. Thank God for the summer house. He passed a police car, already on-site by the drive gate.

*   *   *   *   *

They had an early supper, and started off while there was plenty of daylight. They looked in at the summer house on the way. It was just as they had left it last night, no one had been there since. And now in the daylight, they could see the marks on the wooden floor made by the rollers on the bed, when it had been opened.

Who was it that needed to use this place?

"It certainly wouldn't be a member of the Ferguson family, it's been more recently used than that," said David thoughtfully.

"With all these bits of leaves and dust, it's hard to say how recently it was used. Anyway, the Fergusons had their own house to use," Kate said.

They could see their path of last night well defined. But then it could have been like that for years, as no undergrowth will grow under beech trees.

They pushed through the hedge into the lane, and walked along it in the opposite direction from last night. There was a fresh breeze, already it was tossing leaves from drowsy trees. They were beginning to litter the lane. Straw was caught on the bushes from passing harvest wagons. Brambles crawled over gaps in the hawthorn, the chalky lane was as untidy as a tousled room. The sinking sun threw long blue shadows over the gold-green of the downs.

"Whatever we do or do not find, isn't this a glorious walk?" David said.

The lane petered into a bridle path that wound round the lower slope of the down. On either side of them the down-land sward was woven into the flowery threads of purple bugloss, golden ladies bedstraw, and the wild spotted orchid. They looked down the valley, and could see it bathed in the blue haze of evening. Gradually, the path swung round towards the village, then quite suddenly it finished at a gateway in a high stone wall.

"Now wait a minute. This must be the wall enclosing the park around the Manor House," David said.

The gate was locked but they could see the continuation of the path through it. It went straight through deep woods carpeted with foliage, then out of sight as it dipped down the hill.

"Who lives there?" Kate asked.

"A family called Gresham. The bloke is the local Tory MP. I don't know any more than that about them, but do you remember the village church was full of their family memorials, and stained-glass windows, presented down the years? You know, the usual squire touch!"

"Oh yes, and Grandpa's ashes in a marble urn. I remember."

"All that scene goes on in these parts. They might even 'call' on us one of these days — that'll be a laugh. Or perhaps the Rector and his lady will ask us to take a glass of Madeira at the Rectory, to meet the Squire and his family."

"This is quite a new world for us, isn't it David. Especially after Hampstead."

"Yes, but I can remember this sort of thing going on when I was a kid, when we lived in Salisbury. Tradition don't change much in this part of England, there's something very basic and lasting here. I wonder if, subconsciously, that's what made me want to leave London and apply for that vacancy in our firm in Salisbury, when we got married."

"P'raps. But let's get back to this, I've got hung up on it now. I can't think that these aristocratic Greshams would want to use our tatty summerhouse. So..."

"So?"

"It must be someone who has nothing to do with either Beech Farm, or the Manor, or their families, but who knows it's there."

"And who reached it from the lane, and pushing through the hedge. Let's leave it now to the police, shall we?"

"It probably has no connection with that... thing.... in the well, at all. But what a blessing Marion Ferguson left when she did. It's a ghastly thought that she'd be alone in the house, while all the time some strange character was using her summer house, and even sleeping there — and I'll bet up to no good."

They met no one as they walked back along the lane, it was hardly used. In the silence of the evening, their steps seemed to echo from its hard flint surface. The sun had slipped below the Downs, and it left behind a scarlet sky, slowly fading in the West.

4. __The Inspector at the Manor house__

Inspector Williams bustled into Salisbury Police Headquarters. He was on the job, and had not noticed the clean, sweet air of the morning. That thin nose of his, that smelt out decoys and twists before they showed themselves, was on the scent, and twitching.

He opened the door into his office, threw his hat onto a chair, and called out "Sergeant, is that autopsy report out yet, on the body in the well?"

"Yes sir, just arrived. I've put it on your desk."

Sergeant Frank Turner stood to one side and watched the Inspector as he read the report. Just the job! It was time he earned a bit of promotion for himself. Turner was a burly square-jawed six-footer. He was efficient, keen, ambitious, and prepared to work as hard as Inspector Williams would drive him, and this was an Inspector known for driving his men as hard as he drove himself.

Then Williams said aloud, "death by drowning about four months ago. A woman aged early 30s. Traces of hair found to be reddish. Marks of identification: a plain wedding ring, and a large solitaire diamond ring on the fourth finger of the left hand, a gold Swiss bracelet watch on the left wrist, a pearl necklace with diamond clasp." He turned to Sgt Turner. "Well?"

"Just so. So, we look among the prosperous for missing persons."

"We've got one tailor made on the files Sir, and from Larmer Magna village."

"Who?"

"Mrs Amanda Gresham. Reported missing four months ago, wife of John Gresham, of Larmer Manor, Conservative MP for South Wilts."

"Fetch me the file, Sergeant."

Sgt Turner stood in silence beside the Inspector while he studied the file on Amanda Gresham. He knew better than to volunteer further information, until his superior was ready.

"Who interviewed Mr Gresham at that time?"

"I did, Sir. It was his opinion that his wife had lost her memory, and was wondering in the country. We sent search parties and tracker dogs, and police were alerted all over the South. Hospitals and Accident Admissions were all notified to report. We've found nothing so far, Sir."

"Oh yes, I remember now, a lot of press headlines. I was working up at the Yard at the time. And there's never been any trace of her?"

"None whatever, Sir."

"Why did Mr Gresham think she'd lost her memory?"

"She was under medical and psychiatric care, had been for some years. She suffered from sudden outbursts of violent temper, kind of brain storms. When they had subsided she became mentally confused, with little memory of what had been happening. She seemed to be a lady of wilful and irresponsible behaviour. She had had one of those attacks immediately before her disappearance."

"Poor chap! Well Sergeant, you'd better get him on the telephone, and put the call through to me. He'll have to come and see if he can identify the jewellery."

"Yes Sir."

"The site is completely sealed off, is it?"

"Oh yes, Sir. I've got a man on duty there, Constable Cope of Larmer Village."

"Right! I'll wait here until you put Gresham through to me."

Sergeant Turner hurried off, a gleam in his eye. Still... I bet it'll end up with just a suicide he thought, as he dialled the number of Larmer Manor House.

*   *   *   *   *

"Can't think why any woman who lived in such surroundings as these should get tantrums," Williams murmured as he looked at the graceful charm of the Manor House.

"It wasn't just tantrums, Sir, it was an illness," Sgt Turner said at the wheel of the car.

"Well, let's get this interview with Gresham over. Poor chap was very shaken when he identified the jewellery — that ring was their engagement ring. It was a real grief, not simulated. You don't usually fool me."

"Probably just suicide, Sir, while her mental balance was disturbed."

Williams raised one eyebrow. His grey eyes became deliberately vague again. "Perhaps," he said coolly as they both got out of the car.

They went up a flight of shallow stone steps, and rang the bell beside a heavy iron-studded oak door. An elderly man servant opened it.

"Mr Gresham is expecting us," Williams said.

"Yes Sir, he's waiting in the library for you. Come this way."

As they shook hands, Williams noticed the deep lines around this man's wide sensitive mouth and long nose. Too deep by far for a man of 35. His brown eyes were dark with strain.

"I'm sorry to intrude at such a time as this, Mr Gresham, but it's all part of my job, I'm afraid."

"Of course, Inspector. Fire away."

"You've met Sergeant Turner before, haven't you?"

"Yes indeed. Do sit down."

"I'd hoped to have better news than this for you Sir, after all our enquiries," said Turner, taking his cue from his superior. There was something biting the Inspector, he wasn't usually as gentle and concerned as this.

"Could you tell us the last time that you saw your wife?" Williams asked.

John Gresham's face flinched. "Yes. It was after breakfast on the day of her disappearance. You know about her outbursts from time to time?"

"Yes. I'm told she was under medical treatment for it."

"That's right. She couldn't help it you know, any more than you can help having measles. She had had one of her attacks the day before."

"What did you do, when she had them?"

"Try and persuade her to take the sedative bills that the doctor had prescribed for these occasions. She wouldn't always take them, in fact she often threw the bottle at me. I treated her as soothingly and gently as I could, reminding myself all the time that this was a symptom of her disease. And of course, I always let her doctor know. If it did get too bad, he'd come and give her an injection, that quietened her down. But the attack always wore itself out. She was very quiet after it, drained of energy."

"What happened on this occasion?"

"Oh, it took its usual pattern," he said wearily. "I'd just got back from London, and found her in the midst of it. By the evening it was beginning to calm down, so then I took myself for a walk over the downs to get away from it all — I often do that. It rested me and helped to get things back into perspective again. This country gives you a special kind of strength, Inspector."

Williams nodded understandingly. "And then?"

"I looked into her bedroom on my way up to my own room, just to check she was all right. We have slept in separate rooms for years, you must understand. She was asleep. Next morning when I went in to see her, she was sitting up in bed having her breakfast. The storm hadn't quite passed, she looked at me in a glowering, unwelcoming sort of way."

"What did you do?"

"Nothing really. Just told her it was a beautiful spring day. I remember telling her that. It must have been the last thing I ever said to her. Then I went straight out into the estate farm office, to clear up estate business that had piled up while I'd be in London sitting in the House, where I'm an MP."

"Did you stay there all morning?"

"Yes", he said emphatically. "Even stayed on there for lunch. When I got back here about teatime, the housekeeper told me my wife had gone out during the morning, and had not yet returned."

"So, you went straight from the Manor to your farm estate office after breakfast. And you never left it until you returned to the Manor at teatime?"

"Yes, that is correct."

"You never went out during the day at all — you are absolutely certain about this?"

"Yes, absolutely. When I got back here, hearing my wife was still out, I went to see if her car had gone, but found it is still in the garage. So, I assumed she'd gone to walk off her mood. And she was on foot, and could come to no harm."

"Did she'd often do that after an attack?"

"No, only very rarely. But she had been known to do it."

"When did you start to worry?"

"When it got dark and she still hadn't come back."

"What did you do?" asked the Inspector.

"First I phoned her doctor and told him. He came here to the house, and waited with me for a bit. We didn't want to make a fuss, in case she'd just lost awareness of the time. She was often very vague after an attack. But when she still hadn't turned up in another hour, we phoned the police in Salisbury, and the Infirmary, and the Cottage Hospital in Shaftesbury."

"Why didn't you let Constable Cope know? He was in the village."

"With respect, Cope is a very nice reliable lad, but a slow thinker. I wanted something done, and quickly."

Bang goes any promotion for Cope in the future, thought Turner, as he wrote all the points of this interview in his notebook.

"And after that, the search spread all over the south, with no results until four months later... two days ago."

"Yes, Inspector." John Gresham dropped his head into his hands. After a while he raised his head and looked Inspector Williams squarely in the face.

"You had better know now, as part of your inquiry, that I stand to benefit financially very considerably by my wife's death. She and her brother shared a large family fortune which was entailed. I believe at her death her share is divided equally between her brother and myself. We had no children. She was very rich, but very beautiful too." These last words were spoken in nearly a whisper.

Inspector Williams glanced at the full-length portrait hanging on the wall over the fireplace. He saw a perfectly moulded face with high cheekbones, and pearly skin; wild blue eyes, and a cloud of marigold coloured hair. Her pointed chin had a cheery cheeky tilt to it. How lovely she must have been. How easy for this strong looking handsome man, to love somebody like this.

He looked round the room with its shelves of leather bound books, its oak panelling, with deep window seats below Tudor lattice panes, with Persian rugs on the polished oak floor. Yes, it was a mellow gracious room, smelling faintly of leather and cigars. Not many of these left as private family homes now, nearly all Electricity Board Headquarters, or children's homes, or whatever. Perhaps her money had something to do with its upkeep.

He looked back at the portrait. It dominated the room for him now. She must have taken this historic house by storm when she arrived as its new young mistress. Her pretty figure frisking in and out of these rooms, her light step speeding over the oak floors, running over those wide lawns in and out of the ancient cedars, a dazzle of freshness and young beauty waking up the whole place. Her laughter and gaiety must have sparked new life out of these old stones.

Then he looked at the dark brooding man opposite him. They must have been a marvellous couple. Such a tragic end to such a brilliant start. He felt John Gresham's hopelessness, weighed heavily on his own shoulders. He roused himself. "What about her brother, Mr Gresham?"

"His name is Ashley Wentworth. He is her twin brother, aged early thirties. A bachelor. Lives in London in Belgravia," he told Williams abruptly.

"You don't like him?"

"We're different types. I am a countryman basically, he is a city man. Our different interests bore one another."

"Did the late Mrs Gresham get on well with her brother?"

"Oh, they were devoted to each other, got on like a house on fire. That was the trouble. After they've been together she'd fly into some of the worst of her rages. I always knew we were in for a bad time after their visits to one another. It must be that he over-stimulated her, she had always had an excitable nature right from the start, before there were any signs of this mental illness to follow. That was part of her beauty... she was so vivacious, so vivid... she outshone everyone, the whole London scene. Everything about her was vital."

It was beginning to ring a bell now. "Wentworth... weren't they the city banking family?" Williams asked.

"Yes, that's right. Sir Roger Wentworth died and left his fortune divided among his two children, that is to say my wife, and her twin brother Ashley."

"How did Ashley Wentworth react when she went missing?"

"Oh, he came down here in a towering rage, similar to her own outbursts, only not quite so bad. He blamed me for the whole thing, almost as if... as if... I had murdered her."

"What did you say to him?"

"I reminded him of her illness, and that it was a hereditary complaint. I did discover that, Inspector, when I first took her to a doctor. They searched into her case history before making a diagnosis. Her mother had died in a mental home when Amanda was a little girl. Probably Amanda herself never knew that until then. Ashley was so unreasonable, it was no good talking to him. So I ended up by ordering him to leave my house."

"Have you heard from him since... this discovery?"

"Not a thing. And I wrote to him telling him of his sister's accident. Anyhow, he must have already known from the press reports. I only hope he doesn't turn up at the inquest and cause trouble. I am a sort of figurehead for these parts, and possess the respect, and I hope affection, of the country people all around. My family have been here for four hundred years".

"I shall have to get his London address from you. We shall have to interview him as part of the routine enquiry."

"Of course. I'll write it down now."

As he handed the slip of paper to Frank Turner, Williams said, "well thank you Mr Gresham. We won't be bothering you again yet awhile, though I'll have to come to you, probably later on, for still more details. We'll inform you immediately of any developments."

"I'll leave it all in your capable hands, Inspector. And thank you, it has helped me to talk to you."

John Gresham walked them to the front door. In spite of his grave face, his eyes were clearer.

5. The detectives at Beech Farm

"Drive up to Beech Farm next, Frank, we'd better go and question the chaps working on the sewer trench up there," Inspector Williams said.

Frank Turner looks quickly at him. Williams' voice usually so brisk and practical, was quite different — almost as if he was shouldering the squire's burdens himself, and he could see an abyss ahead. It sounded dangerous to Frank. The squad had always trained their men to regard crime as crime, and no police officer worth his salt let himself get emotionally involved with any of the suspects. This case may not be crime, or on the other hand it may. If it was, then everybody associated with the dead woman could be regarded as suspect, until the tangle had been unravelled. He certainly wasn't going to let the inspector get himself mixed up, by relaxing that code of non-involvement if he could help it.

"Okay," Frank said. "Constable Cope will be on duty there right now, we could have a talk with him too."

"Good. He'll be able to give us a bit of a lead on these village characters. We need that." A degree of briskness was back in the inspector's voice, to Frank's relief.

They drove up the village street, and stopped the car at the Beech Farm drive gate. When they got out and looked back, they would see beyond the village a view of interlocking hills to a distant horizon. The only sounds to disturb the sleepy stillness were the drone of combine harvesters, and the lazy cooing of pigeons.

"It gives you the feeling of being miles away from civilisation," Williams said under his breath.

"Well we are eighteen miles away," Frank said, still engaged on keeping the inspector's attention occupied with the enquiry. Imagination was all very well in its place.

Williams laughed, and they opened the gate to go in search of the two workmen. They found Bill and Ernie digging a trench near the house, as the drive gate area was temporarily sealed off. They stopped work as the two detectives reached them.

"Can you come up here for a few minutes? We want to ask you a few questions," Turner called down to them in the trench.

Bill and Ernie looked at one another uneasily, wiped their hands on their trousers, and then clambered out of the trench. They all then sat on the grassy bank bordering the length of the drive.

"It was you two chaps who uncovered and dismantled the well top down there?" Williams asked.

"Yes Sir, we be them," Bill answered.

"Both of you?"

"Yes Sir."

"Will you both think back very carefully to exactly how you found it. How you uncovered the well and dismantled it. It's very important that we get these details in the right order, only you two can give them to us. It must be absolutely accurate, so just take your time," Williams said.

Neither Bill nor Ernie needed to do that. They had earned many free pints at the Kings John's Arms the last two nights telling their story — nothing like this had ever happened in the village in living memory. It made all the scandals of poaching, and illegitimacy, look like vicarage sew-ins beside it. As the evening wore on, and the fug in the bar thickened, tales about Mrs Gresham grew wilder. Every village person had feared her, including Jimmy, who had learning difficulties. He was often seen shuffling after her, his rolling eyes fixed on her, as if fascinated by terror, yet no one quite knew why.

"We be digging this trench see, up the road from the village, used a pneumatic drill first on the road," Bill said.

"Yes," interrupted Williams, "I mean after you started work inside the drive gate on the Beech Farm property."

"Ah well, it be all digging therre, the ground be so soft, see," Bill said.

"So, you dug from the gate along the line drawn by the Water Department, in the direction of the house?"

"That's roight. About two yards in beside the drive, would you say Ernie?"

"That be 'bout roight," Ernie said, as he took off his cap, and scratched his head.

"Were there are lot of leaves over the part you had to dig?" Williams asked.

"Leaves Sir? Must 'ave been a good foot of leaves, would you think, Ernie?"

"That's roight."

"It be all of them trees down there. An' the chestnut, must 'ave seen a few 'arrvests, must yon tree. We just shoves the leaves to one side, then we see a great leaf-mould pit under the trees a few yards away, so we shoved 'em into it," Bill said.

"Then you started digging," Williams encouraged them, almost sorry he had ever mentioned leaves.

"Aye, that be roight," said Bill

"And you dug down pretty deeply," Williams said.

"O' courrse! That be a sewer, bain't it," Bill said, pronouncing his astonishment at such ignorance in an inspector.

"How deep would you say?"

"Same depth as a sewer o' courrse."

Williams gave up this line of questioning, he knew defeat when he heard it. "When did you hit the well?" he went on patiently.

"When we see that bit o' corrugated buried 'neath them leaves. We found it sticking out, see, just a bit of corrugated. We chuck it to one side, then there be this couple of well doors under it, all rotted like, and broken in."

"What were the well doors like?" Frank asked here.

"Loike? Loike well doors, Sirr." And to think they're supposed to be smart in the CID an' all.

"Can you show them to us?" Williams asked.

"They be down there under yon trees. Bob Cope's standin' over 'em, as if they'd be made o' gold, not just rotten bits o' wood an' old hinges."

"They're like trap doors that meet in the middle?" Frank persisted.

"O' Courrse," Bill used the tone he used to his two year old son.

"We'll go and inspect them later. Now, you say they had rotted in the middle?"

"Aye. Got a darrned great hole in the middle," Ernie suddenly made his contribution to the conversation. He had stopped scratching now, but judging by the puckering of his face, the art of concentration was clearly a great effort.

"What did you do next?" Williams asked.

"Chucked them rotten old doors out the road, then us broke down the walls of the well like, to level with us trench. Us be waiting till foreman come to give us orders about filling in the well. We looked down, and saw the body, see," Bill said.

"Could you see it was a body straight off?"

"Not straight off. It looked summat be there, an' it bain't water. But all wells be low just now, this dry summer, see, the springs be down. So I calls Ernie over. 'Ernie' says I, 'Can ye see what that be?'"

"That's roight!" Ernie broke in; this was ground he knew, performed in the pub. "I tells Bill it looks like a sack of summat what someone's chucked down. An' Bill says 'More like a body'. We takes another look, and Jeez, 'e be roight!"

"Then Mrs Fletcher come down from the 'ouse, and she sees it too," Bill added.

"So, let's get this right starting from the top layer. First there were the leaves. Next underneath them, was a sheet of corrugated iron. Below that were the rotted well doors, with a hole in the middle of them. Below that was the well itself. Right?" Williams said slowly and carefully.

"Yes Sirr," Bill said. "That be roight," agreed Ernie.

"We'll go down and have a look at them now. I wonder where the corrugated iron came from?" Williams said.

"The leaf pit, o' courrse. Folk do that in these 'ere parts, chuck a spare bit o' corrugated on top o' them when ye get them raked into the pit, stops 'em from blowing back, see. Makes lovely mulching for the garden, cuts like butter when it be real rotted," Bill explained to these rather ignorant detectives.

Williams was beginning to wish he hadn't told these two characters to take their time. "It was just a sheet of corrugated iron like that?"

"Aye." Bill was growing accustomed to these two townsmen.

"So, you would say nobody could fall into the well with the corrugated iron over it?"

"No Sirr. It be quite safe like that."

"I suppose at some time it must have had a winch and cable over the top, for winding the buckets on."

"Aye. That be lying in the leaves. Fallen over wi' rot. Must be a couple o' years since it be used, and even then they might be a bit rotten like. The Colonel let things go a bit at the end."

At this point Kate Fletcher came out to them with a tray load of tea and biscuits. "Good morning. I thought you'd all like a break," she said. Her smile was like morning coming up over the hills, and thoughts of corpses in wells drifted away.

"That's very kind of you. I'm afraid we must be a nuisance, wandering in and out of your garden like this," Williams said.

"You can't help that. It's a wretched thing, but I try and keep my mind on how lovely it's all going to look in the spring, when this miserable business is over."

"It does that," said Bill. "All these banks, and down there 'neath yon trees, covered, real covered, with daffodils. It be real pretty. An' before that, it be all covered in snowdrops, masses o' them, in the woods an' all. Gypsies come and pick 'em to sell in the towns. It be a sight for ye. Ye'll be arrl roight, when this be over." Bill knew she would be, such a bonny lass, it made his groping for words more difficult. Foreigners expected words from a bloke, village folk knew what you meant, when you just spat.

*   *   *   *   *

As he stood guard over the well, Bob Cope's immobile dark blue and silver figure waited for the two detectives. He knew it was his turn to be interviewed. This was likely to be the awful moment of his career, just as he was tired too, after being up night and day guarding this lot.

He lived in the village in the police cottage with his mother. She herself was a police widow. Bob had attended Shaftesbury Grammar School, where he had achieved a steady, plodding and unspectacular record, except for boxing for the school. Automatically he joined the police force, his ideas stemming entirely from his mother, of whom he was her pride and sole occupation.

The village of Larmer Magna knew him as an easy-going friend, rather than an enforcer of the law. And it was surprising how he looked just a lad, like any other country lad, when he took off his helmet. But it didn't matter whether he was checking licences, or poachers, or the young Jack from running up the village street in socks newly knitted by a harassed mother, Bob Cope's understanding, and slow polite authority, could be relied upon.

He knew more about what went on in Larmer Magna and district, then he ever let on. He knew when not to look over his shoulder. He also knew that his country folk had their own codes and rules, many of which sprang from Gypsy Lore, gypsy blood ran in much of their ancestry. He never interfered unless called in to do so.

He always felt awkward and shy of his superiors from police headquarters. When they appeared, the confidence of the serene uneventful pattern of his days was thrown into confusion, uncertainty, and a longing for them to shift off. After all, he and his people knew and understood one another, these superiors from outside understood nothing about any of them. Bob didn't want cases he could measure his wits against. He didn't want promotion. He did want just to be left alone, to enjoy the quiet of the life he knew.

He licked his dry lips. Now a respectful uncertain smile cracked his solid country face, a face that had listened for the bleat of sheep through the milk mists. The two detectives came up to him.

"Constable Cope?"

"Yes Sir."

"Let's have a look at these well doors, and the sheet of corrugated iron, and that rotted winch and chain."

After they had examined them, Sgt Turner measured up the size of the rotted hole in the well doors, and the whole area.

"Strange how the well opening should have been at ground level, instead of having a stone parapet round it," Williams said.

"A lot of them are like that round here, Sir," Bob told him. "The circular doors on the top of the well, are much bigger round than the rim of the well itself. They open upwards from the centre. There's no need to build parapets round it, the well doors couldn't drop inwards."

"So if you wanted to push anything into the well, you'd have to lift the doors upwards first," Williams said slowly.

"Yes Sir. You have to do that before you can run the bucket down on the chain."

"So, this rotted hole in the well doors may not be connected in any way with the corpse falling into the well?"

"No Sir," Bob sounded surprised. "Happen the wood just rotted under that corrugated iron, from the moisture coming up from the well."

"Yes... yes... could be," said Williams thoughtfully. "Anyhow Cope, there'll be a car coming round to collect these exhibits before the Inquest, for the Forensic Science Department, so have them ready."

"Yes Sir."

"Now can you tell me something about the local people, who knew and had contact with Mrs Gresham?"

"We all knew her, Sir."

"You knew her fairly well yourself?"

"Not more than others. She was... well..."

"Yes?" Williams encouraged.

"She was a lady who had very queer turns, as you might say. We all knew that, even Jimmy."

"Why do you mention Jimmy? Who was he?"

"He has learning difficulties, Sir. His father, old Tom, was Colonel Ferguson's gardener up here at Beech Farm. Old Tom worked here every day. He drew the drinking water from the same well, I've seen him doing it every day for years. Jimmy, his son, used to do odd jobs his father set him on to in the garden. He could do quite a few useful things, in spite of being how he is."

"Where's old Tom now? Can I see him?"

"Oh no, Sir. He died just before the Colonel died, pneumonia it was for both of them, in that hard winter."

"Who drew the drinking water from the well then?"

"Jimmy mostly, for the short while Miss Marion stayed on here. He could, you see he'd helped his father do it enough times. Some of the rest of us, myself too, came up and gave her a hand with things as well. It was no place for a lady on her own. But we were all sorry to see her go. Everyone round here liked her."

"Why?"

"She was kind, helped a lot of folk in the village when they needed it. She was a smiler too. She'd been brought up here, looked after her father when her mother died. You hardly ever saw them apart, he seemed to depend on her a lot — that's a fact, he did. They were grand together."

"What about Jimmy? Is he still in the village?"

"Yes. Still lives in the same cottage with that mother of his — she's a right one! Vicious old gypsy! You'd see him as you walk down the village street, Sir, he's always leaning on his cottage wicket gate, sort of lolls over it, with his mouth hanging open. His eyes roll a bit. He's got a bad squint too, but he never misses a thing that moves up the street. Poor chap!"

"Can he speak?"

"Only in a funny sort of way, more like grunts and animal noises than words. But old Tom and his mother knew what he said, the Rector seems to as well, so did Mrs Gresham."

"How did Mrs Gresham come into it?"

"I'm not sure, Sir, how it started. She was always walking about with her Airedale dogs, and a riding crop in her hand. Jimmy was frightened of her, quite a few folk round here were, that's a fact, they were. Then one day her two dogs set on him down by the pond. He was lolling against a tree at the time, looking at nothing, the way he does. These dogs suddenly went for him, and there was Mrs Gresham shouting and yelling at them, and beating them off him with her riding crop, darned nearly killed them too, she did."

"But Jimmy came out of it unhurt?"

"Sure. But after that, wherever she went, even if it was just walking over the Downs with the dogs, Jimmy was always following her a few yards behind. Sometimes she chased him off with her riding crop, you'd see the poor devil shuffling off as fast as he could shuffle, looking over his shoulder, his eyes rolling as if the devil was after him. Then sometimes she'd just let him follow, all according to her mood."

"Did she talk to him at those times?"

"Not exactly talk. She'd shout back a few remarks at him over her shoulder now and again."

"What sort of remarks?"

"Things like telling him to pick up his feet, or wipe his nose. Or he could call at the Manor for some apples. All sorts of things. And when he grunted at her, she seemed to know what he said."

"It'd be no good for us to interview Jimmy?"

"Oh no, Sir. You'd never understand what he said if he spoke. Like as not he'd say nothing at all, just keep looking at you with that vacant sort of squint. He'd never understand neither, what you were asking."

"Bad as that, is he?"

"Since birth. He must be about twenty now. Old Tom idolised him. He's only got that mother of his now, she doesn't bother with him, poor chap. She comes from the gypsy stock round these parts."

"Your local knowledge is very helpful, Constable. There is a lot more you can tell us about these people, and we do need to know. So, make a list, and give details of all those who were in any way associated with Mrs Gresham. I want you to build up a really good dossier on them. Think it out, even to the smallest detail. It's often the details that lead to the clues. How do you think yourself, that this lady landed in the well, Constable?"

"Darned if I know, Sir," Bob said unhappily.

6. Kate meets people in the village, and has a visitor

It was afternoon when Kate walked down the village street to the shop. She was running low in tea and sugar. The white cottages basked in the afternoon sun. Blue bottles were zooming over cow pats on the road. A pity, she thought, that an early Victorian brewer should have built that hideous red brick pub in the middle of all this. Even the trees round it looked as if they were angrily clenching their roots in the chalk soil.

As she pushed open the shop door, she found herself the object of curious stares, from three silent women. They seemed to crowd the little shop. Yet she had the distinct feeling that her entrance had abruptly stopped a very close, and confidential, discussion.

"Good afternoon, Ma'am," said Mrs Marsh from over the counter. Strange how this "Ma'am" and "Sir" routine still went on here, just as it had done down the generations. Kate felt just as foreign here, as she would have done on the Chinese border. The other three women still eyed her silently.

As Mrs Marsh wrapped up the tea and sugar she said, "It's bad luck for you to have... trouble... like that so soon after moving in, an' that's a fact".

Mrs Marsh's tone brought the whole menace nearer. It was dragging it straight into the shop, especially when the other three women joined in with "Aye, it be." The afternoon became heavy, even the air sweated.

"My husband and I feel like that too, it makes me wish we'd never come to Beech Farm. We are just hoping the police will soon clear up the mystery, then we can set about forgetting it all."

"Aye, and it's a queer feeling that anyone coming into my shop could be that other one."

"What other one?" Kate asked.

"That one of the police are looking for. We've known everyone here for so long, you see, all our lives. With all the funny ways folks have, there's not one I know would do that."

Kate looked around the village shop. It had originally been the front room of the cottage. Its shelves, and the one counter, were loaded with the conglomerate needs of a community, with just enough space for an archaic weighing machine, and for the customer's head to look through. Black boot laces were next to the sliced bacon, detergents and furniture polish jostled the farm eggs. Liquorice Allsorts and chocolate, rubbed against the cheeks of cheddar cheese and corned beef. At the end was the Post Office counter, chiefly manned by Mrs Marsh's eldest daughter, Nancy. The musty smell of packaging, peppermints, stale food and dry rot, never altered through the seasons. The shop vied with the Snug at the King John's Arms, for being the centre of village intrigue and gossip.

Kate's tone was deliberately casual when she said, "it was probably only an accident. The police are just trying to establish that it was one, I expect."

The three women looked at her. "'Appen so," one of them said.

"Well I'd better be getting along," said another.

Kate watched the three gnarled women with wispy grey hair, walk away. They looked like the three witches, she thought. She could just see them through the shop window, in a gap between the notice announcing the Fete in the Rectory Grounds next week, and the monthly meeting of the Women's Institute. A jam jar containing vinegar, was full of the day's captive wasps, a buzzing mass of seething dying struggles.

Mrs Marsh's pale eyes watched her with compassion. She was only a slip of a girl really, not much older than her own Nancy. It was a shame.

Everything about Mrs Marsh was pale, from her indeterminate thin hair which had once been fair, to her complexion yellowed with anaemia from too much child rearing. She had once been a pretty parlour-maid at the big house, in the next village of Chettle. Then at the beginning of the war, she married Able Seaman Harry, on one of his leaves. Harry was the postman now, and owned a van. He was the younger son of a local small farmer, and though he no longer farmed, he rented a field off his family. There he kept a cow, a couple of pigs, and some hens. His cottage garden was so well manured by his cow and the pigs, that he was a regular winner of the vegetable prize in the annual show.

"If my Harry can give you a hand with anything up at Beech Farm, you only have to let us know," Mrs Marsh said kindly.

"Oh thank you. So far we are all right," Kate felt less of a foreigner with this gentle woman.

"He's real handy whatever he sets himself to, he was a sailor in the war, and sailors learn to be handy, don't they," she'd said proudly as if 'The War', the Second World War, had been only yesterday. "But he is never free on a Tuesday or a Friday."

"Oh..." Kate said, knowing some answer was expected of her, so that Mrs Marsh could launch into explanations.

"Yes, you see he goes into Bournemouth on Tuesdays and Fridays with his van. He takes all the rabbits what the village have snared, and sells them to the market there. He takes the Rector's flowers too, to one of those smart new hotels on the Front."

"The Rector's flowers?"

"Oh yes. He grows beautiful flowers, and wins prizes with them too, in those big London shows. He ploughed up the five-acre field, and turned it all into flower growing. That big hotel near the pier in Bournemouth, buys them off him twice a week. My Harry stacks all the flower boxes in the back of his van, along with the rabbits, and in the winter there are the… birds too, 'o course," she laughed. "I bet Bob Cope knows just where they are poached from, just as well as the lads that do it. Still, Harry'd be glad to help you on any of the other days."

"We'll remember that, and thank you."

"You might just meet him coming up the street, he should be on his way back now from the Rectory. He's just been up to remind them at the Rectory, to pack their daughter's mackintosh in time for the parcels collection. She's been here on holidays, and left her mac behind, there's a card from her this morning, asking for it. When Harry read it while he was doing the postal round, he knew they'd forget about it up there, unless he went up and reminded them. He knew Miss Angela wouldn't have sent the card, unless she needed it badly."

"Does he always read people's cards, before he delivers them?" Kate gasped in astonishment.

"O' course. It's the way it's done here. Can be useful too, like my Harry reminding them about Miss Angela's mackintosh. She put a P.S. on the bottom of it for him, hoping his foot was better, he'd a bad heel when she left."

Kate was bereft of words.

Mrs Marsh added thoughtfully, "the police won't find it easy if they start questioning village folk. There is a lot goes on here, that all of us know about, but nobody tells. I'll bet Bob Cope won't be much help to them either, he's one of us, you see."

Kate walked home. In spite of the hot afternoon, she shivered. The village was like an ebb tide uncovering hidden stretches of a strange, closed-in community, that she and David had had no idea existed. She could hear the lonely bleat of sheep from the hillsides. Trees whispered secrets and threats from dark copses. Shadow and light chased one another across the down slopes, but the deepest shadow stalked beside her, as she passed the well at the end of her own drive.

It should be only three hours now, until David got home, and tomorrow was Saturday, then Sunday... perhaps she'd have got more used to all this by Monday, when he had to leave for work again.

*   *   *   *   *

When Kate reached the house she saw an angular grey haired woman ringing the front door bell. She looked a flat heeled tweedy type, only on this hot day she wore a sensible tailored linen dress.

"Oh, Mrs Fletcher, I'm so sorry to butt in on you like this. My name is Pendleton — Canon Pendleton's wife from Lamer Rectory."

"How nice to meet you, do come in." It was sheer relief to find her here at this moment. She had been dreading solitude for the next three hours, with racing thoughts taking charge. This woman had a serene smiling face with calm grey eyes, that made her feel more normal, in a normal world again.

"I'm afraid this is rather a casual way of introducing myself, but we've been so busy of late, there doesn't seem to have been any time," Mrs Pendleton's easy laugh chased away some of the shadows.

"It's all right, I'd rather have it this way. David and I are not formal people, we hate it. My name is Kate, by the way."

Kate drew her into the sitting room, and could feel the horror sliding away.

"Oh, isn't this a charming room. You both have done wonders with it. This lovely bright blue against such pale grey walls. Your bowl of orange marigolds in the corner, is just the right touch. You clever girl!"

Her enthusiasm warmed Kate. "Would you like to come over the house, and see what else we are doing with it? It'll look even more different by the time we've finished with it, we are going to spend the winter decorating, and doing quite a bit more alterations. David's an architect, and full of ideas, and knows how to do these things. It's a good thing he does, as it's much cheaper to do it ourselves, especially as the money is running a bit low after paying for the house. It could have been fun to do it…"

Mrs Pendleton heard a wistful note in her last words. She said with a cheerful voice, "I'd love to see it, I adore houses. And old ones like this are the greatest fun. You can read the whole of life from them, because they're part of it."

"Yes, I felt that too. But it can have its disadvantages," Kate said quietly. Mrs Pendleton looked at her enquiringly, but asked no questions. By the time they got back to the sitting room, they felt they had been friends for some years.

"Do you ever get lonely here, Kate?"

"Not till this afternoon. I've been so busy, I haven't had time. I felt a bit grotty when I got back from the shop, and thank goodness saw you here."

"You won't when you start having babies."

"I know. I'd like to start soon, but David doesn't want them yet. So I guess I'll have to wait a while."

"Well, next time you feel lonely, just pop along to us. I had three like you, the two girls would be near your age I should think, but my son Richard is quite a bit older.

They're all away from home now, so you can imagine how delighted we'd be to see you, dear girl. You're the sort of girl that would muck in with whatever we are doing, so don't forget. But tell me, why did going to the shop make you feel lonely?"

"It's all this business over the body found in our well. I felt a sort of menace closing in on us, David and me. We've put everything we've got into this house, it's what we'd dreamed of. Now it seems smothered in tragedy and gloom, I'm wishing we'd never come. David doesn't want to leave it now, but I do. And we were going to be so happy here, grew roots, build a good family life, and have fun."

"And you will too, dear Kate. Don't worry, it will all part, and become another dot in its history. The inquest is to be held on Monday. What a blessing that the Coroner has decided to hold it in Salisbury and not in the village, that helps quite a bit." Kate remained silent, fighting back her sudden tears. Mrs Pendleton continued, "but I know what you're feeling. It wouldn't be quite so bad if you'd lived here for a bit of time first, and it's so awful not to know. Even a definite verdict of murder would show us where we stood. The village is full of whispers at the moment, that's why we thought we'd carry on with the fete just as planned. Normality puts things back into perspective for people. And that's really what I came about in the first place, until I got charmed by you, and it chased the fete out of my mind."

"It's mutual," Kate said.

She laughed. "Now don't side track me from the fete, dear. It is in aid of the new heating for the church this year. We would like you and David to help. It will be held a week tomorrow, that's Saturday next week, in the Rectory grounds. It'll be the usual drill of the flower show, flower arrangement competitions, vegetable stall, side shows like Aunt Sally, bow and arrow contest, guessing the weight of the cake and the name of the doll, find the hidden treasure, and later on dancing in the barn — the full works! That brass band will be coming over from Berwick St. John, to blow their way through Pomp and Circumstance, and The Merry Widow."

Kate laughed.

"That's better." The calm grey eyes looked relieved. "I want you, dear, to help with the flower stall, and David with Aunt Sally. Apart from fete activities, it'll be a good chance for you to meet all the locals. They turn out in a body for this sort of thing, even if they don't go to church, it's an occasion. So will you do it?"

"It's not really our scene as you've probably guessed, but yes, we'll have a go."

"Good girl! You will find you have to adjust to all sorts of different ways and things here, it's all part of village life. When you come to live in a place like this, you have to become part of the community and its activities, or miss out on the whole scene and remained a foreigner in every way," she said vigorously.

"I felt one today in the shop."

"You most probably did. But you're very sweet, they'll accept you. You will have to give them time, though. The more you help in the village activities, the shorter the time will be. A good tip is to involve yourself with them and their welfare, they're rather like children. As you give them the chance to get to know you, their suspicion of 'the foreigner' will slide away. Dear Marion Ferguson was genuinely involved and concerned for each of them. For that alone they all still miss her. But of course, it was easy for her, she was born here."

"I'm very curious about her, we seem to have her quoted at us such a lot. We only met her once, at the solicitor's office, when we signed the contract for the house. As you see, we've all this lovely furniture that she left behind."

"Yes, I recognise it."

"Why did she make this impact on people?"

"I think it was because she was very warm-hearted, and completely kind, and that's rare. She was brought up here, then went away to school, then to Oxford where she got her degree. Pity was, while she was there her mother died of cancer. So instead of the world being her oyster, as it is with those of your generation, she lived at home here with her father, and motored into Salisbury every day, to teach English in a school there.”

“But she was happy here. You should have heard the way she spoke of it, we could hardly bear it for her.”

“Oh, she loved this place, and the people, and this house.”

“So why was it a pity?” asked Kate.

“Well, it gave her a very narrow environment. She ought to have had a greater breadth of experience. I rather gather she turned down marriage for the sake of her father. Those two were very close indeed, I don’t think she could have brought herself to leave him. The tragedy is that in the end, he left her. Dear Marion! Life must be far from easy for her now. I don’t mean financially, I’m sure the Colonel would have seen to it that she was left comfortably off — but in adjustment. These village people were the world to her.”

“Yes, that’s the impression we got.”

“She worked very hard at the last general election, helping John Gresham win his seat, he is our Tory Member of Parliament. She became his right hand man, I think a lot of his votes were due to her efforts, he’ll miss her at the next election. Whenever anything was needed, whatever it was, Marion was always at hand to do it. She became completely involved with it. So much so, that after the counting of the votes in Salisbury Town Hall, when he was declared the winner of the South Wilts seat, she suddenly burst into tears in full view of all the party workers. She must have been completely exhausted, poor child."

"You'd have thought his wife would have done some of that work."

"You wouldn't say that if you knew his wife. She wasn't even there to see his triumph. The nice thing was the way John got Marion a chair, and gave her his handkerchief, and kept standing and patting her shoulder, until he got her smiling again, before he went out onto the balcony, to receive the Cheers of the crowd. We could hear them all cheering, and calling for him, while he was comforting Marion, I'll never forget it. They made a good working couple."

"What about John Gresham's wife? After the discovery in our well, it concerns us too now."

"Poor old John! He was a sorely tried man for so long. He really didn't deserve this sort of thing to be round his neck, after all those years of loyal care for that tedious woman."

"Was she completely barmy?"

"No. that was the pity of it. If she had been, one could have felt sorry for her. He could have put her in a home, and perhaps led some sort of life on his own. She had these lunatic attacks, alternating with relatively normal spells, but she was a headache even in those. Poor John, I don't know how he stuck it. Only a man like him could."

"What sort of headache was she?" asked Kate.

"The kind that any thoroughly spoilt selfish child is, that needs disciplining," said Mrs Pendleton vigorously, and then laughed. "I'm afraid I always boil up when I think of that woman, I'm sorry! Her trouble was that she was born rich, and was the centre of admiration. She thought the world was created for her whims, to be trodden on as it pleased her, peopled by twits who were there to jump to her commands, even the Rector and his wife!" She laughed again. "I'm glad John's free. Perhaps when this menace is all over, he can start living again."

"He must have been fond of her though, to go through with it for so long. Surely they'd have got divorced if it was that bad?"

"Oh no. You will understand when you know John. He was more her father and guardian than anything else, he became so anyway. If they'd split up, she'd have had nobody to lean on, before, during, or after her attacks. No one else bothered with her, except that brother of hers, and he was useless. He was nearly as crazy as she was too, but not quite. He had more cunning about him. No, she'd have gone haywire without John, and he knew it. He's the sort of person who'd never have forgiven himself."

"It sounds a pity he didn't marry Marion Ferguson instead."

"My dear, he must have been all of twenty years older than Marion. She was a kid at boarding school, when he married."

"What a mix-up, isn't it. Seems so unfair, and in this lovely village too. The wrong wife, insanity, death, loneliness..."

"But it's true of some lives in any place, isn't it?" said Mrs Pendleton, wisely.

"I suppose so. But it's not going to be true of our place, at Beech Farm."

"No, well it doesn't apply to most people in Larmer Magna either. Anyway, John has been very sensible and sublimated into lots of different interests, apart from his Parliamentary work. He's involved in all these digs in the district, on the Roman camp sites, and on Ancient British settlements. Once you get him on that subject, you can never get him off it."

"Oh, I'm so glad. David will be thrilled. That's his great hobby too."

"I'll see that they get together as soon as possible. Heavens! Look at the time! Gossiping like this to you, and there was a pile of things waiting for me to do yet."

"I've loved it. I'm getting to know my village through your eyes."

"Well dear, we'll see you then on Saturday week at the fete — two thirty at the Rectory. But let's meet before that. Could you both come up for a drink on Sunday morning, after church, to meet my husband? We'll ask a few of your neighbours along as well, so that you can get to know them, and John Gresham. We can brief you and David then, on your fete duties."

"We'd love to come. But there's just one more thing," said Kate. "Who was the Little Grey Lady, that I've heard spoken of in the village?"

"Oh that," said Mrs Pendleton laughing. "Some of the village of people think they've seen an apparition of a Little Lady dressed in Grey eighteenth century clothes, with a grey bonnet and shawl, and a long dress, in their garden. But she is always very benign, and seems to bring happiness to the people who see her. They think she's probably the soul of someone who lived very happily in this village, two centuries ago. But I must go. We'll much look forward to seeing you and David, on Sunday morning."

Kate watched her active slim figure hurry away with decisive steps, and started to feel safe again.

7. <u>Sunday morning at the Rectory</u>

On Sunday morning David and Kate woke to see a fierce downpour of bad-tempered rain, so on David's insistence they had breakfast in bed, and then idled the morning away together, until it was time to get up and dress to go to the Pendleton's at midday. He knew this kind of loving could bring her happiness and contentment again, in the environment of this house, that she was mentally running away from now.

The day before he had chipped away the plaster and brick from that wall in the hall, and found his guess had been right. Gradually, he had exposed an open fireplace, some hundreds of years old. As he stood back and gazed in wonder at the soot-blackened stone and brick round the old hearth, and saw even the iron hook still in place, where ancient metal stew pots had hung, he had experienced one of the most thrilling moments of his life. He had called to Kate excitedly, to come and share it with him. She had joined him reluctantly, glanced at it, and then said coolly, "I'm surprised it is only the fireplace that was blocked up. I'd have thought they had been at least one skeleton hanging on that hook," and then walked away.

His excitement plummeted into deep disappointment. She seemed to have dismissed the house, and everything to do with it. It looked as if any further work on it would have to be done solely by himself. Beech Farm was driving a wedge between them, where none had ever existed. Yes, this way of spending Sunday morning could be the best medicine for her, the work on the house could wait.

By the time they were ready to set off for their walk to the Rectory, the clouds had broken up in a rinsed blue sky. Butterflies and bees flew out to enjoy the sudden warmth, though the trees and bushes still dripped heavily. To get to the Rectory, they made a short cut through the churchyard. They passed ancient tombstones, among ancient yews, on a steep slope of fresh rain-washed grass. For so many generations that stone Norman church, with its squat tower, had heard the same hymns sung by the same families, in the same Dorset/Wiltshire brogue, sounding not all that different from the bleating of their sheep on the surrounding Downs.

Mrs Pendleton met them with a warm welcome, and led them into a big drawing room, with the sun streaming through long windows, onto gay flowered chintz curtains and covers. There were great bowls of flowers placed in the house, at every eye-catching point.

Kate said "I've never seen such gorgeous masses of them like this, wherever you look."

"They're all grown by my husband, you know. You've heard about the Canon and his flowers, I expect?"

"Yes, Mrs Sharp at the shop told me. They are wonderful, and so beautifully arranged. It must take you all day doing them," said Kate.

"Oh, I only do the little bowls. He does all the rest himself. He's really very good at it, isn't he!"

"He's certainly artistic," David said.

"Come over and meet him. I've told him so much about you and Kate."

They liked the Canon instantly, liked his scholarly face, under scanty white hair like a sprinkling of fresh snow. His bright robin eyes were gentle, and never stopped twinkling. He had strong square shoulders, evidence of his Oxford rugby and rowing days. He had a great roar of a laugh, which filled every corner of the house, and even of the Salisbury cinema, where he never missed a Peter Sellers film, if he could help it. But compassion creased his face as much as laughter. You could say anything to this man.

As well as John Gresham, they found the doctor, a farmer, and a young solicitor and their wives, had all been invited to meet them.

John Grisham came straight to David. "The Canon tells me you're interested in ancient history and archaeology."

"Very. You're just a man I want to meet. I've read about the digs round here. And I believe you've had scale models made of them, and they're in a small museum somewhere. I'm so interested in what you're doing, this is a great centre for Roman camps, isn't it?"

Together, they drifted into a corner, to talk of their mutual interest.

Kate watched them go. David's head, topped by that mop of tawny hair, that firm sculptured chin with a slight cleft, he was such a hulk of a man, looking even more so in his polo neck sweater. A pang of pride shot through her, also a pang of pity. It was tough what she was putting him through, but somehow, she couldn't stop herself. In spite of all, his love was so tender. She must try and control this unaccountable bitterness. She had never experienced anything like this before, she felt as old and tough as Beech Farm. If only they could leave it and its treachery, she knew things could be all right between them again. As she looked at him, she felt that old catch in her breath, it tightened her throat.

She looked curiously at John Gresham, a man with a decided presence, and an unconscious air of authority. He had those dark closed-in sort of eyes, that told you life wasn't much fun. Yet, seeing him now engrossed in archaeology, it was hard to realise that the Inquest on his wife was to take place in the morning. Kate couldn't help watching him out of the corner of her eye, while trying not to appear too bored with the dumpy Scottish Dr Macdonald, and his equally dumpy Scottish wife. They talked of nothing but their prize chrysanthemums, grown personally by the doctor in his greenhouse.

They were talking in a group with Mr and Mrs Bennett, the rosy-cheeked farmer and his plump wife, who had a laugh like the bang of a gun, which when it took Kate unawares, nearly made her airborne. When the topic of chrysanthemums had been exhausted, Mr Bennett asked her if she was interested in horses, and riding to hounds.

"No, I'm afraid I know nothing about them. In fact I'm usually nervous at the back end of a horse," she giggled, then waited for the shock ripples.

Mrs Bennet almost snorted, "perhaps it's both ends of the Kings Road you are more at home with."

Yes, even the gentle wild flowers would cower under their leaves, as that lady strode past them down the lanes, Kate thought. Then she looked up to find Mrs Pendleton at her side.

"Kate darling, I want you to meet these two nice young Lloyds. They live quite near, in the village of Farnham three miles away. They've got a lovely old cottage that they've done up, you two would have a lot in common."

By the time Kate had finished with Jane and Trevor Lloyd's tennis and otter hunting in the summer, mixed hockey and beagling in the winter, and the Fergusons — oh yes — the Fergusons, her curiosity had won. She found herself drifting over to David and John Gresham in the corner.

David slipped his arm round her shoulders as she joined him.

"This is my wife, Kate. Do tell her about those tree clumps."

"I was just telling David that you probably both noticed those formal tree clumps, on the tops of the ridges of the Downs, here and there."

"We have. We wondered how they got there," said Kate.

"They were planted as a commemoration of the sites where the beacons were lit, to spread the news of victory over the Spanish Armada."

"Everything you see here has a story behind it," Kate said. The minute the words were out, she could have kicked herself.

"Yes...", John Gresham said slowly. "I hope you have many happy years at Beech Farm. I'm sure you will, it's a happy place."

"Was it a happy place when the Fergusons lived there?" David asked.

"Indeed it was. There was a lot of peace there, and love. He was a splendid old boy. A typical product of the days of the British Army, serving in the outposts of the Empire. A great man, in many ways."

"And his daughter?" David asked.

"She was brought up in that atmosphere, alongside him, and of course it brushed her too". He changed the subject. "If you like walking in the country..."

"But we do," David eagerly interrupted.

"There are wonderful walks here. You will find you're always walking precipitously up the hills or down them, never on the level. But when you reach the top, it's worth every panting breath. It's like walking on the green roof of the world, while great Downs and valleys roll away as far as you can see. There's nowhere quite like it."

"You make it sound as if there isn't," Kate said.

"It's my country," he said simply. They were all three silent. Then he went on, "in time I can show you some wonderful places. The Quakers' burial ground is worth walking to. It's still maintained by the Frys, even though it is hidden in a wild folded valley in the centre of the Downs. You can only reach it to this day, by a five mile path through a winding valley, then suddenly you come upon it. It can be seen from nowhere, that's why it made such a perfect hiding place during their persecution — only the rabbits and foxes knew its whereabouts. The Canon conducts a service there on behalf of the Quaker dead, every year."

"They fled to this area did they, during those times?" Kate asked breathlessly.

"Yes, you see we are so perfectly hidden among our Downs, and of course in those days even more so, as the present roads were just bridle paths then, except for the Roman road from Salisbury to Blandford. Your Beech Farm was owned by a famous Quaker called Rideout, he gave refuge to many."

"And does the Canon conduct that service out of doors, all among the Downs?" Kate asked.

"Yes, with the land gulls circling above, and the larks rising singing into the sky. And there's the sad little railed-in spinney, hiding the Quaker graves. It's one of the loveliest occasions you could attend. You must come next year, I think you'd both appreciate it."

"It's fascinating. We had no idea!" David burst out. "You must come and see us, and tell us all you know about it."

"In time, in time. But not for a while yet. You understand?"

They nodded. That was the only reference he made to the findings at Beech Farm.

*   *   *   *   *

"Isn't it extraordinary, David," Kate said as they walked home, "there's that inquest in the morning, over one of the greatest tragedies this village must have known, in spite of its history. And there they all were, sipping sherry, and talking as if tomorrow morning was just like any other Monday. Not one of them referred to it, except John Gresham once, in that oblique sort of way. Yet it must have been uppermost in everybody's mind."

David laughed. "That's yer-actual-British-bit. There's a lot of that around here."

"What will happen at the inquest?"

"There'll be a formal evidence of identification of the body, and the pathologist report on the cause of death, that's about all at this stage. John Grisham will of course have to be there, and the various police on the job. That's about all the Coroner can do at the moment."

"What happens while the police are ferreting around?"

"Nothing. If after a bit they have reason to believe it is murder, but haven't yet charged anyone with it, then I believe the Coroner re-opens the inquest with a jury, who return a verdict of 'Murder by Persons Unknown'."

"But suppose they've found someone to charge?"

"Then I think the Coroner just issues a Certificate of Death for the relatives, and all the rest is dealt with by the Assizes. I believe that's how it works."

"We won't have to go to the Inquest, will we?" asked Kate.

"I might pop in myself just to see what's going on. The workmen who found the body and dismantled the well coverings will have to be there, so there'll be no trench digging in the morning." He glanced at her, then took her arm. "I'll take you out tonight to a slap up dinner in Bournemouth. Tell you what, let's go to that hotel decked out in the Rector's flowers, and hang the expense."

"I wonder... I wonder did the Little Grey Lady belong to the Rideouts? Was she his wife, or his daughter?" Kate said softly.

David laughed. "Hey, you are not starting to believe all that guff, are you?"

Kate didn't answer.

8. <u>Marion Ferguson comes to Nottingham</u>

Marion Ferguson looked round the sitting room of her Nottingham apartment. Yes, she had made it very attractive and comfortable. As she looked out of the window, she could see right over the quiet tree-lined roads of the Park. On a summer's day like this, the air was filled with the sound of rustling leaves, and birdsong. You could almost imagine you were living in the country.

In the country.

It seemed a lifetime since she had left it. She would never go back now. Her life was here. She was carving out an interesting niche for herself. She had got this job as an English Lecturer at the University, within an easy car ride of her apartment too. The work was absorbing, among a whole new set of people in the University, people who shared the same interests as herself. She was learning to direct the Drama Society. She was an active worker in the local Conservative branch. She was making a lot of new friends. Yes, this new life was becoming satisfying. Satisfaction and interests were a good substitute for happiness.

It had taken some doing though.

Two years ago, she had lived in that tedious little apartment in Salisbury, teaching English to school GCSE strugglers. All right, Salisbury was old, the house her apartment was in was old, but so was her spirit. Living on the brink of a life that was ended, and could never be snatched back.

It was after an evening of self pitying tears, that she made the decision. Next morning she felt light with relief, after she had given in her notice to that School Head. It was good to be free. She's scanned the educational vacancies, anywhere at all was suitable, so long as it was not in the vicinity of Larmer Magna. In fact, the greater the contrast to Larmer, the better.

She remembered now, the sparkling June day when she drove up to Nottingham for her interview, for that job at a College of Further Education. What a break it would be to teach school leavers, at A level standard.

She arrived early, so drove around the city a bit, to see what it was like. She had never seen Nottingham before, and now it started to excite her. This stimulating integration of new with the old. This could be her scene, and she'd go all out for the new, a complete break with the past. This place was alive with urgency.

She sang as she drove back, not from happiness, but from a determination to find happiness in a different form. She'd spent the night in London, then back to Salisbury the next day, to finish her last term there.

*   *   *   *   *

"Say goodbye to it, Dinah-girl", she told her miniature Dachshund bitch, sitting on the passenger seat beside her, as she swung the car away from Salisbury. "We're going north to Nottingham. We won't be coming back here, we don't want to, do we!" she said it firmly enough to convince anyone.

Dinah stood up on her hind legs, and rested her front paws on the side window ledge, and looked out at the houses sliding past — at the life she and Marion had known, sliding past. As they reached the open road, she dropped down, smuggled against Manion's leg, and rested that long nose across her lap, gazing up at her with her fixed stare of adoration.

Marion dropped one hand from the wheel, and stroked Dinah's head.

"We'll be all right Dinah-girl. We can talk to each other, can't we." Who was comforting whom?

*   *   *   *   *

The only thing to do on arrival was to book in at a quiet guesthouse, until a decent apartment could be found.

The guest house overlooked a recreation ground. Inside it smelt of the herrings that they had had for lunch, and the sprouts now cooking for dinner. The manageress showed her up the brown painted stairs, with its narrow strip of thin Axminster carpet, to a back bedroom overlooking the kitchen yard. It was a narrow room, with just enough space for the bed, a wardrobe, and a cheap brown painted chest of drawers, that served as a dressing table. But they had agreed to allow her to have Dinah in here with her, and in the lounge, as no other place had.

The manageress said "I'll send a man along to bring up your luggage. Dinner is served at seven," as if it was the Savoy, no less.

"Don't worry, Dinah-girl. It'll do until we find our own place. It won't be for long," Marion said as if it was really Dinah she was encouraging. But Dinah didn't need comfort, she was far too busy snuffing around the room, snorting into corners, then standing in the narrow space between the wardrobe and the bed, wagging her tail, and letting out short questioning barks.

Marion gathered her up, hugged her, and buried her face in the warm furry neck. Dinah looked smug with contentment. After a while, Marion raised her head, blinking her eyes. "Come Dinah, let's decide where to put your basket, where there is least draught." It was a deliberately cheerful tone.

After dinner, she took Dinah for a walk. She needed a breath of fresh air, after that seedy lot in the musty dining room. There were a couple of travellers, looking at her with interest, obviously reckoning whether she would be good for a night out. The other guests seemed to be middle aged residents, with their own private sauce and mineral bottles at their elbows, a drab, defeated looking bunch. How strange it was, never to have actually seen this kind of greyness before, yet it had all been there. While she finished the meal, she read a paperback crime novel she had luckily brought with her.

It was better once term had started. The college was one of those modern glass buildings. The staff were friendly, and her work at a more interesting level. During work hours Dinah stayed in the car, snuggled up in her blanket, and in the lunch hour they went for a walk together. After tea, Marion stayed on in the library, preparing the next day's lessons, until it was time to drive back, to that watery tasteless dinner in the stale dining room. Afterwards, she would take Dinah for a walk, then returned to the library to correct books. She was happier there; fortunately the place was open, because of evening classes.

Now the Golden Rule was broken. She no longer insisted on Dinah sleeping in her own basket, but had her curled up close to her, on the bed, under the eiderdown.

And often in the night, as she turned over, her fingers would be feeling for Dinah. When she felt that smooth, welcoming, warm head and neck under her hand, and Dinah giving her fingers a sleepy lick, then she would drop off to sleep again.

During that first term, she watched the local paper for advertisements for apartments. She went the rounds of the estate agents, but never found the one she felt she could really settle in, make her home. Part of the trouble was, not knowing enough about the place, so she couldn't decide which district to choose. But the right apartment would turn up — it must — things did sometimes. Meanwhile, the guest house was convenient for college, and it was easier just to drift on.

Near the end of term, Canon and Mrs Pendleton wrote and asked her to stay with them for Christmas, but she refused. Later, one Saturday morning, she received a letter from John Gresham, inviting her to spend a fortnight of her holiday over Christmas at The Manor. He wrote, "Amanda would be nearly as pleased as I'd be, if you came. She only said at lunch today 'she would do us both good, see if you can't persuade her to come.' I'm not just persuading you, sweet Marion, I'm begging you to come..." She slowly put the letter down. Tears threatened to overcome her.

She stood up suddenly, her face set with determination. She looked down at Dinah who was wagging her tail, her ears cocked, with that asking expression in her eyes. She swallowed and shook her head, as if shaking away the misery.

"All right, Dinah-girl, we'll drive out to what's left of Sherwood Forest, and walk hard. We'll tramp all day, until we nearly drop." Marion quickly got ready for the day's outing, almost blind in her haste. She turned her tears to the wind.

*   *   *   *   *

She spent Christmas in Oxford, staying with her only Aunt. Widowed Aunt Margaret was so like her own mother had been in many ways, she never interfered or asked questions. She just looked after her, and was ready to listen, if that's what was needed. She hardly ever thought of her mother now, but Aunt Margaret brought the memories surging back. Her own mother had been much the prettier of the two sisters.

And Oxford turned out to be a good choice. Quite a few of her old undergraduate friends were still there. One or two had taken higher degrees, and had jobs at the University, others had their homes there. It all turned into a pleasant gathering, and helped to strip away the dreary thoughts.

"You're mad to waste your time in a fiddling job teaching A-levels. I've heard that Nottingham University has some sort of crisis, and are looking for a Lecturer in the Department of English," one of them said. "Why don't you apply?" And another from her year said "you've got a good MA degree, the right sort of personality, you're even pretty, you'd walk it, dear girl."

But somehow, she didn't feel like making any more changes yet. She seemed to lack the incentive and energy, for making that kind of decision. Then, to her joy, Richard Pendleton, the Rector's son from Larmer, turned up out of nowhere, on Boxing Day.

"Whatever made you come, Richard?" She'd never felt so pleased before, to see his square shouldered figure, and grey eyes that held his serene smile. He was such a safe person.

"My parents told me you were here. I thought I'd come and see how Miss Independent Career Girl was making out. Pity you didn't come and stay with us."

"It was a sweet invitation from your parents. Was Christmas just the same at Lamer?"

"Just the same."

"Mrs Bennett bossily organising the church flowers."

He laughed. "Just the same. Ma's as tactful as ever with her, and leaves her the field."

"And the carol singing?" asked Marion.

"Yes, the carol singing. We all missed you."

"Throssle Willy led the singing, and Harry accompanied with his accordion, as ever?"

"Yes, but this year we all practiced round the piano, in the King John snug, as there was no Beech Farm to practice in," said Richard, poignantly.

The fun it had been! She would never forget it. Her memory went back to their friendly village group, trudging through the lanes, and over the Downs, to the outlying farms and cottages, singing carols all the way, as well as outside the houses. The men swinging storm lanterns as they all tramped through the woods, what ghostly patterns they made of moving light and shadows, distorting trees into elongated twisted strange shapes, like Rackham drawings. How crisp and frosty those nights were. The sky seemed so clear, the stars looked like big yellow flowers in a navy blue field. And those glasses of home-made wine, and slices of hot lardy bread the farming folk called them in to share, before moving off to their next singing stop.

"Did you still collect for Save the Children Fund?"

"Still did. Nothing changes," he said.

No, nothing had changed. It still went on, only now... without her.

"I remember a young girl who got a bit plastered one year, on all those glasses of home-made wine, offered to us on the round," he teased.

She laughed — could really laugh again. "That's just the sort of thing about the you would remember!   We finished up at the Rectory at midnight with 'see amid the Winter's snow.'"

"Of course. And my parents waiting for us all in the kitchen, with hot rum punch and mince pies, just the same."

"Wasn't it a drag how you were always put in charge of me, when I was first allowed to go out with you all, I must have been about 15 then. Poor Richard! You were always be made to look after me, not by my Ma, but by yours. It used to infuriate me."

"It didn't me. It gave me a lofty masculine superiority, very ego boosting."

"I used to a crawl into bed on Christmas Eve, sizzling with excitement after all that, those carols still ringing in my head as I dropped to sleep, even to last year when we went out, and I was 24 then."

"They've been good times. You should have come to Larmer and stayed with us, you know, and joined in just the same this year. Why didn't you?"

"I just couldn't, Richard, that's all," she said crisply.

"It's just like you to change your mind suddenly, the minute you find you're selling it. It'll pull you up sharp, and make you realise, you can't be without Beech Farm after all. That's the cussed sort of way you're built."

This was how he had talked to her, ever since she had been a small child. It warmed her, to hear it again.

He went on: "you never know, you might even be cussed enough to marry me one day. If you did... I'd still be waiting." She heard the echo, and the question, behind his banter.

She said quietly. "It wouldn't be fair if I did. Don't wait, Richard dear. You should be married. Lots of girls must fancy you, it's time you looked them over."

When he said goodbye to her, he lifted her chin and examined her face. A faint smile twitched on his upper lip. "In spite of all your efforts to become independent, you've still got that wide-eyed saucer look of wonder, damn you," he said.

He didn't know that every moment of Christmas, as her thoughts reached back, longing for Larmer, Marion discovered that longing can be a physical pain.

9. Marion's apartment, and teaching at Nottingham University

It was lucky that Marion hadn't realised then, that the most difficult time was yet to come. What made that January and February so difficult? It had always been a good time of year at Larmer, however cold. But now she felt like a paper boat at sea, tossing and anchorless.

Her misery even made her late for college one morning.

She woke to hear her alarm splintering the air. She could see pallid morning fringed with grey through the window. Another empty day. Doing a boring job for the sake of the money it earned, part of the life sludge slithering through another year. She felt for Dinah, and tucked her close against her, under the sheet, and cuddled her. As Dinah's cold nose nuzzled her, she closed her eyes.

On this day, hollowed out of winter, in February, pale green spikes of the first snowdrops would be thrusting through the chalky soil of Larmer. In dark silence copses, their scattered whiteness could just be seen. At first they were like tight drops, small as seed pearls squeezed through narrow ducts, like tears. Then they'd spread into sheets of bloom, quivering in the cold wind. You could imagine the joys to come then, when sounds of bees, and of cutting machines filled the air, and the cooing of sleepy doves, snapping of tree branches, hoots of owls, and the flop and flutter startled birds.

She dropped off into a light sleep again, and dreamed she was indoors at home, by a huge log fire. It projected shadows of oscillating ballet on the drawing room walls. Those long curtains were drawn. There was a soft glow of lamp light. And the happiness of watching her father and John, sitting by the fire, bent over their chess board, and while the night wind moaned 'SNOW' round the house.

In her dream she felt the contentment of one day sliding into the next, unnoticed. She could see the way the snow became alive, sculptured into strange sweeping shapes by the bitter wind. And those jewel-rimmed ice-laden puddles, cracked and scarred by her running feet. The way the winter frost crumbled rotted vegetation back into the soil and tidied up the year.

She opened her eyes. What was another spring these days, since all of it must pass, and come again?

She looked at her clock, and leapt out of bed, giving poor Dinah the shock of all time. Dinah let out a jaw-cracking yawn, gave an enormous stretch, shook herself, and jumped off the bed and joined Marion, who was gazing out at the rain.

Dinah wagged her tail, and gave a little bark just to remind Marion that she was awake now. "Look at the rain spurting down, Dinah, like the tears of men," she said in a stifled voice. "Heavens, look at the time! We can't possibly make it up now, so don't let's try. And you know, Dinah-girl, I don't even care!"

*　　*　　*　　*　　*

That evening, when she returned to the guesthouse, she went straight up to her bedroom, closed the door, picked up Dinah, and sat with her on the bed. Dinah was all set with that darting tongue, for a right good licking session.

"No, Dinah. Down! Now listen, we can't have any more of the miseries like the last few weeks, and this morning. You see, I've got no friends here, and I don't think I'm likely to have while I'm teaching at this place. The staff are all Nottingham people, with either their husbands, or their own houses and friends. To put it plainly, except for you, I'm bloody lonely. I didn't know how difficult it would be to find friends, when you're new in a big city. So we've got to alter things, I'm quite decided." Dinah gave a sharp bark, this was the sort of answer expected of her.

"I'm glad you agree. So, I'm going to take up the suggestion they made to me in the Christmas holidays at Aunt Margaret's, and look for a job in the English Department at the University here. People there will be from all over the place, not just from Nottingham. We'll have the chance to make some friends, and have more fun. What's more, I'm going to tell the Manageress of this dump, that I'll be leaving at the end of March... and that will make us have to find the apartment we want, and no mucking! See!"

She gave Dinah a big hug. "So it's going to be interesting, isn't it. And that's the end of the misery! It's taken me all day to arrive at this."

She got up and went to the mirror, combed her short fair hair and flicked it round her face. She repaired her lipstick, smoothed on a bit of eye shadow, and then swung round to Dinah, who was gazing at her with her head got on one side, with that questioning look in her eyes. Did all of this mean and imminent walk?

"No. It's just that it's the new me, preparing again for a new life," she told Dinah. Then down they went for what passed for 'dinner'.

*   *   *   *   *

So now, instead of aimless walks with Dinah, going from one lamp-lit street to the next, they walked round the residential districts like Mapperley Park, Woodthorpe, and Wollaton, looking at houses converted into apartments, and small modern bungalows. But none of them fitted. They were city bred and neat, too much suburban prosperity. Those oblong gardens, separated by neatly clipped hedges from the next tidy oblong. No, she wanted to settle in surroundings that had some character. Then someone at the College told her about The Park. It had once been the ancient deer park to Nottingham Castle. Now that sounded better.

She drove Dinah to Nottingham Castle, and together they spend much of Sunday morning wandering around The Park. This was where, about 100 years ago, wealthy lace manufacturers had built their mansions, on parkland leased from the Castle. Many of the original trees of the Deer Park, still grew here. The gardens and the roads were full of big forest trees. It was an oasis near the city centre, still elegant with lovely old gardens, and mellow brick walls. At the entrance to The Park, is 'King Charles Steps'. This flight of steps up a small mound, just opposite the Gatehouse of Nottingham Castle. At the top of these steps, King Charles I raised his standard, at the start the English Civil War in 1642. The street nearby, leading up to King Charles Steps, is called 'Standard Hill'. Queen Anne's garden is still kept as a garden, among the houses.

Many of the mansions in The Park, had now been converted into apartments, but they had been under careful City Planning Authority control, so that the outward appearance of this unique place is unaltered. This was steeped in character and history, part of the history of Nottingham. This was just what she had looked for. This was where she would choose to live.

"So, all we have had to do now, Dinah-girl, is to go to the estate agents that specialise in Park property and tell them we want an apartment there. If possible a top floor apartment in one of those big converted houses. The view from there must be fantastic, it would do everything for us, even on a grey February day like this," a day with shivering fingers, but with the promise of spring to come.

*   *   *   *   *

April was an exciting month. She was offered a Lectureship at the University starting next October term. And she moved into her apartment in The Park. Dinah was ecstatic, with sniffs and snorts over every inch of it; the sitting room, bedroom and kitchen, her sharp claws slithering over the tiled floor of the bathroom. But her short, busy barks conveyed approval.

The Easter vacation passed in a flash of furnishings, matching up colour schemes of carpets and fabrics. She broke right away from antiques, and let herself rip on contemporary Scandinavian furniture, set off by an olive-green fitted sitting-room carpet, and white walls. She used tangerine lamp shades and cushions for contrast. She had taken special care over the lighting, cosy warm lighting from standard and reading lamps. It had all cost a lot, more than she ought to spend, but it was worth it. This was her permanent home now, wasn't it? She had kept her bedroom elegant and feminine, pale peach pinks on an oyster white carpet, and a lush satin buttoned bed-head. And what a view there was from there.

As she sat at the kidney-shaped dressing table in the window, she could look right across the city of Nottingham. A view of factory chimneys, church spires and towers, nearly all with their heads in the clouds. Glass buildings, stone buildings, and brick buildings, rose out of a grey urban sea. And beyond, the woods and fields of the Trent Valley stretched to Leicestershire. The Trent itself, wound in and out of the scene, like a silver snake. In the mornings, from her bed, she could see the sunrise behind the sharp outline of Wilford Power Station. Then it would touch the city roofs and chimneys with red and gold, before moving traffic and people came out onto the streets. It was a wonderful way of starting her day.

She did all the interior decorating herself. When she needed a rest, she would gaze at her view over the city. The daffodils would be in full bloom at Larmer now. How generous was the spring with that old garden, those sheets of golden trumpets tossing in the breeze on the banks, in the grass, even reaching to the Beech Farm Copse.

She picked up the paintbrush and got on with the job, as if time was chasing her. And anyhow, all of this, this apartment, was hers. It was looking nice too. It seemed a long time since she had lived with nice possessions around her.

*   *   *   *   *

Well, Richard Pendleton had been proved wrong about her natural cussedness. When it came to selling Beech Farm a year later to that nice Fletcher couple, she had not changed her mind. She had had a traumatic visit there, it was true, to sign all those documents of sale in the solicitors office, but afterwards she had driven back to Nottingham as quickly as she could. She couldn't get back here quick enough.

And that was four months ago, now. In that time she had schooled herself to shut out every thought of Larmer and its people. She could never bring herself to see the place again, it belonged to a dead past. It must no longer exist. The future was here, in her apartment, in her work, and her new friends. And nowhere else.

Dinah yelped for breath, at being hugged so fiercely.

*   *   *   *   *

Except for those nerves of hers all through this summer term, this year as a lecturer at the University had been better than expected. But now she had developed this sleep problem. She lay awake for hours, counting millions of sheep, deliberately blocking her mind to stray thoughts. She came to know the silhouette of Wilford Power Station very well, it's black dense mass against the luminous night skies. All those strings of lights along the ring roads, glittering like glass eyes.

She wanted to sleep, yet dreaded the moment of dropping off. It was those two recurring nightmares that terrified her, always the same. She would dream she was being flogged, could feel the whip lashes cutting across her back and ears, slashing round her neck, then drawing tight, suffocating her. Fighting loose, fighting to breathe, and trying to shield her head with her arms, from that flailing lash. She woke then in the grip of terror, to find her own arms tightly curled round her head. Then she lay wide eyed in the darkness, looking for the Power Station's black mass, fixing her eyes on it, to prevent her from dropping off to sleep again. As soon as dawn lightened the sky, and she got up to make herself a cup of tea, she could see Dinah's eyes watching her with reproach, for disturbing her cosy snuggle under the eiderdown.

Another time she would be running. Running away from the sound of padding feet chasing after her, with a deadly threat. It was dark and cold. Her heart pounded into darts of pain that filled her chest. Then she'd hear the heaving breath of her pursuer, running up behind, gaining on her, close behind her now. She'd wake suddenly, to hear Dinah whimpering, and knew that those pounding hissing breaths had been her own. She lay gasping on her pillow, and hugged Dinah, until her breathing had returned to normal.

She got increasingly tired as the term wore on. In the lunch hour, in warm weather, she often went out onto the campus and lay under the trees, where she would flake out into a deep blind sleep. It restored her and gave her the energy to complete the day. She felt too tired to be hungry, but she ate because she knew it was the sensible thing to do. Life had to keep on going, like the grey traffic in the streets.

Then came the end of term concert, with a performance from the University Orchestra. The music department had a high standing. She was listening with closed eyes to the beauty of a cornet solo, when suddenly the cornet slid up to play a prolonged top G. It sounded like a scream — a scream ripping through her head. She had to get up and leave the hall quickly, knowing that if she didn't, she too would be screaming. Friends hurried out after her. "You all right, Marion? You look pretty ropey. Here, come and have a drink."

But she sat and rocked backwards and forwards, crying. And she didn't know why she cried.

That did it. Marino went to the doctor with nerves really as raw as an open wound. She had to get rid of this feeling of dithering apprehension.

"I am prescribing some sedative pills for you to take during the day, and some sleeping pills to take at night.

But you must go right away for a long holiday, certainly not less than a month, and better still if you could make it two months," the doctor told her. Then he looked at her in silence for a minute. He said, over his arched fingers, "is there any specific worry you've got on your mind? If there is, it would be better to come out with it. Apart from the therapeutic value of clearing the air, it's a good thing to enlist the help of your doctor, to face whatever it is. Perhaps this could lead you to some sort of solution."

"Oh no. there's nothing like that. I'm just learning to adjust to a different life and environment. But thank you all the same," she said with a trace of hockey field heartiness.

He continued to consider her in silence for a while. "Well, it must be that you've been overdoing it a bit, trying too hard. Whatever it is, a real rest is what you need, away from the responsibilities and worries of your work. I know you're interested in political work, and it is your hobby. But for this holiday don't even open a newspaper. Just go to a remote spot, and rest in limbo where you can lose count of time and plans. It will recharge your batteries. That's all you need. But you need it urgently. Let everything just give. If you do this, you'll come back restored for the October term. Do you think you can manage it?"

"I do. I know just the place to go to."

"Good. Come and see me again when you get back."

She could so easily do it. It was the end of July now, the University had gone down, and wouldn't be up again until the beginning of October. She had the time and the money, the latter thanks to her father.

The sleeping pills that the doctor gave her were knock-outs. Her nights now became deep blissful sleep, without a trace of nightmare, even if she did wake in the morning with her head feeling as if someone had slapped it.

"So, Dinah-girl, we're off to Cornwall for a holiday. What a relief that will be." She hugged Dinah, who showed her approval with short sharp barks, and a lot of licking. "D'you remember our last visit to Cornwall, Dinah-girl? It can't be what last time was, of course, but it's a place where we were happy, isn't it. Happiness will still be there, even though only in echoes. And you know, Dinah, I've become someone who has nearly learnt to live alone. And I'm even beginning to enjoy it." Dinah's soft brown eyes showed all of her understanding, as she sat on Marion's nice warm lap.

*   *   *   *   *

It was sheer relief that made her sing, as she drove towards North Devon. She planned to spend the night there, and so break the journey to Cornwall. The mere thought of going to Coverack, near the Lizard in Cornwall, was a health restorer in itself. It was strange how she turned to that place now, for help when she needed it. She had gone there with her parents for years, and even went there with her father, after her mother died.

The hotel was perched on a headland thrusting out to sea, with a path running down the cliff to a sandy cove below, which had tall craggy black rocks, looking as if they had grown out of the sand, and were ready to walk into the sea. When the tide was full and rough, the spray would smack the hotel windows, as the waves smashed against the cliffs. It felt as if you were out at sea. The hotel owners knew her well, and for so long, they always managed to find a room for her, however short the notice.

The fishing village of Coverack was a mile away, along the shore from the hotel. It had a miniature harbour, and a busy little quay littered with drying nets, coils of rope, stacks of empty fish boxes, and every kind of tackle. Fishing boats and sailing boats rocked gently on the swell. There were fishermen with leathery faces, smoking the kind of Shag that vied with the smell of tar, and of stale beer. White cottages nestled along the line of the shore under the hill. Lobster pots were ready to be thrown into the tide. It was a timeless sort of place, the timelessness that she needed.

10. <u>**The police consider the evidence**</u>

On Monday afternoon, Inspector Williams sat at his desk at Police Headquarters in Salisbury, pouring over the dossier, compiled by Bob Cope. The Inquest was over. Everything had gone smoothly, with no trouble from Ashley Wentworth, the dead woman's brother. It was strange how the man had not even bothered to turn up. The Coroner had pronounced formal identification of the body, and stated the pathologist report as 'Death by Drowning'. At the moment that's where it rested. It could rest there not a minute longer.

That was the reason for Williams' thin anxious face, being so furrowed with fatigue. He had been studying this dossier the whole night, fitting pieces together, and then finding they didn't really fit. Bob Cope had set out all the village people as a dry list of names, and facts, instead of a series of human beings with a life to live.

He leaned back wearily in his chair, and stretched out his legs. He flicked the dossier over to Frank Turner sitting opposite. Williams had called him an hour ago, to see if he could make anything of it. He was a sound chap, keen too, he might have a different angle on it. He needed that at this moment.

"What d'you make of it, Frank?" he asked, and closed his eyes.

Immediately, John Gresham's face swam up behind his closed eyelids. In all his crime detection experience, he had rarely seen eyes so naked and stark with misery, as the man answering the Coroner's questions in a quiet carefully modulated voice. It was horrible. It drove him on at this moment to search for the hot lead he needed, out of this jumble of names. There would be no rest for him, until he had landed the suspect with the evidence.

In the stillness a blue-bottle hummed like an aeroplane and bombed against a sunny pane of the closed window. It fell on its back, on the dusty window ledge, still buzzing.

"This is no good to us," Frank said, irritably. "Seems as if Cope is making it as difficult as he can for us."

"That struck me too."

"Look Sir! He's written up every member of Larmer, and of the nearby villages. It appears every one of them has had some contact with Mrs Gresham, mostly trivial. The only thing that comes out of it, is that none of them are heartbroken to see her go. He's got too many people on it to be of any help, reads just like a parish register."

"Did he do it on purpose Frank? Is Cope doing a hedging job on us? Just an idea of course, but on whose side is Cope working?" Williams gave a tired sigh.

"It's obvious I'd say, he is part and parcel of that darned village. He couldn't disobey your orders, but he's stuck so strictly to the letter of them, that it's as much use as an electoral roll. But the other thing that comes out of it, is that lad with learning difficulties, Jimmy. He was the only member of the community to cry at her death. He was inconsolable four months ago, on the morning that woman was found missing, and that timing ties with the pathologist's report on the autopsy. At that time, the village thought it was just another symptom of the lad's learning difficulties, but he may well have known she was dead."

"That's just it!" Williams exclaimed in exasperation. "Our chief and only witness would appear to be this lad with learning difficulties, who could neither understand, nor speak, but who can see. D'you remember Cope describing how he leaned over his cottage garden gate watching the street, and never missed anything that moved up or down the road?"

"Yup! And later Mrs Marsh at the shop, complained to us about this lad, the way he was always shambling through the woods and the lanes. They never quite knew where he was, or when he was looking at them through the hedges and the trees, a village Peeping-Tom," said Turner.

"Mmmm. But she did add, that all the same he was quite harmless. I'll bet that poor devil knows more about the machinations of those village people's lives, than anyone else. I wonder could he ever be made to speak? It is essential that he should."

"Who could do it? A psychiatrist?"

"I don't think he'd get very far. A strange face frightens the guts out of those sorts of characters. No, it'd have to be someone he knew."

"That, Sir, means the dead woman, his own mother, or perhaps the Rector," Turner suggested.

"It does. His own mother's interpretation of the lad's words would be totally unreliable. According to this dossier, she'd say what suited her, and use it to level up a few old scores. It's the only bit of character study we get out of this dossier, one wonders if Cope is levelling up a few of his own old scores. It's no good. What about the Rector?" Williams pondered.

"We could try him, Sir. They all seen very fond of him."

"I'll phone and see if he could see me this evening."

"Isn't it's time you got off a bit this evening, Sir? You been working on this all night."

"Murder makes its own rules about working hours, Frank."

"You really think it was murder?"

"Looks like it. Let's go back to the beginning and look at it coolly. Before Marion Ferguson left Beech Farm, she had placed a sheet of corrugated iron over the top of the well doors, as an extra precaution, in case of further rotting of the doors. The well contained only water at the time, and that was nearly 2 years ago."

"How do we know?"

"Because she was drawing drinking water from the well up to that time, there was no other source. And the pathologist's report is that the drowning took place about four months ago. Right?"

Frank nodded. "It's best to check off as we go along, Sir."

"If it was suicide, the person would have to remove the corrugated iron first, before either jumping through the rotten doors, or opening them so as to jump in. Right?"

"Yes, Sir."

"In which case, when the workmen came across the well, they'd have found the sheet of corrugated iron flung to one side and would NOT have found it replaced on top of the well doors."

"Right, Sir. And we've checked, and cross checked their statement, separately, together, and made them demonstrate on the site, exactly how they found it. Without doubt, the corrugated iron was found on top of the well doors."

"And there's no motive why they should give a false statement. They live in a different village, 5 miles away, and only knew the dead woman by sight, even Cope corroborates that. So with this, it can't be suicide. Neither can it be an accident. If she had fallen accidentally through the rotten doors, supposing someone or the wind had previously lifted the corrugated iron, and flung it to one side, the hole would have been found open, and uncovered. Right?"

"Not quite, Sir. Suppose it was an accident, and later on some Nosey Parker poking about the empty property, noticed the rotten well doors with a hole in them, and put the corrugated iron over it, not knowing a body was down there?" Turner suggested.

"If that was so, it will come out in the intensive and extensive questioning we are going to do, right from the estate agent, to every child in the village. There'll be sick of us, before we are through."

"Perhaps they'll think of that themselves, and someone will say they put it back, just to get rid of us."

"They may, but I doubt it. These country minds work in more simple direct ways than that. We'll see. But just suppose no-one comes forward with that idea, it clears stage one."

"Right, Sir."

"It's stage two that bothers me. It leaves only one thing. A human hand that pushed the live, or already dead body, down the well, and then replaced the corrugated iron again over the well doors, so that it looked undisturbed. And that is death by murder," Williams concluded.

"The measurements of the rotted hole would fit the measurements of a slim person, she was slim, so she could have been pushed through the well doors."

"And on examination, Frank, the fragments of wood round the hole, were seen to be dropping inwards, splinters of it were found in her clothing. It proves that it was through well doors, that she fell."

"That's right, Sir."

"That could lead to the supposition, perhaps, that it was a corpse pushed down the well, rather than a live woman. It would be difficult to get a live, fighting woman, exactly in position on the well doors — they're not very big. Even if the attacker knew they were rotten, they may not have been rotten enough, so she wouldn't have dropped right in. Then she'd have lived to tell the tale, and that would be too big a risk for the murderer."

"But the cause of death was 'drowning', Sir. There are no streams or rivers in Larmer Magna, because of its chalk soil. The nearest river is about 12 miles away, beyond the Downs. There's only the village pond."

"And that is fed by an underground spring, just as these wells are. Well thought of, Frank. That's true, the chalk like a sponge, sucks up all the moisture, and then drains as rivers and streams out of the chalk, further down, at a lower level."

"No one is going to drown her in the pond first, it's in the middle of the village, in full view. Even if it had been possible, it would mean having to get the body up the full length of the village street, past the cottages, the shop, and the pub, to Beech Farm drive gate at the top of the village street."

"So, the village pond is out. What about drowning her in the bath?" Turner suggested.

"Even so, whether it was by night or by day, if the body and had to be carried there, someone would have seen some movement going on at the end of the unoccupied Beech Farm drive. It's in full view of the whole length of the village street. Don't forget, the men in that village are renowned for their skilful poaching, probably part of their gipsy heritage. I suspect that place from midnight onwards is alive with them. No one could be pushing bodies down wells, without being seen by someone snooping around."

"What about by day when the men are out working, and the women busy in their cottages?"

"It's still in full view of the whole place. And don't forget, this was a deserted property, and had been for some time. So, it'd be common knowledge that no one had any business there, so there'd be instant nosey curiosity, to see what they were up to. This is a closed community, where they all know each other's business, it's their hobby," Turner concluded.

"You're right, Frank."

"So where does that get us, Sir?"

Williams dropped his head wearily into his left hand, and closed his eyes again. "It's what I've been trying to figure out all night," he said. "She died by drowning, presumably down the well. She was pushed down it by a murderer's hand. But how, and why? That leads us back to the dossier."

"Suspect number one I suppose, would be her husband."

"Yes. He's suffered years of her. He stands to gain a lot of money at her death. But if it was he, why should he go to these lengths of the well. He could have found an easier way than that, what with his apartment in London, and Larmer Manor."

"Her apartment in London, Sir. It'll be his now."

"Ye—es. It's too obvious, Frank. It doesn't sound good to me. In him we've got a suspect with a motive..."

"And yet?"

"That's it, Frank. When something is as clear as that, someone has made it so."

"So, you mistrust it?" Turner queried.

"I prefer it to be more obscure than that, let's say. Anyhow, he wouldn't do it on his own doorstep, it's too easy to pin back on to himself. If I was he, and had criminal intentions, I'd have felt more inclined to do it in such a way and place, that it involved other people, particularly perhaps that brother of hers, whom he hates. After all, the brother gains financially too, from her death. According to hearsay, he'd be more the type likely to do such a thing. This death... seems quite out of character, for a man of John Gresham's calibre."

"He may have suddenly snapped. He'd been under great strain for a long time. There's no telling when a snapping point comes in a man. He doesn't plan or reason, in a sudden crisis."

"He must have got used to that particular strain, learnt to live with it. That was obvious when we interviewed him. If his nerve was going to snap, it would have done so a lot earlier than this."

Frank looked at him with one eyebrow raised, but kept silent. He drew his feet back under his chair, making a scuffing sound. The bluebottle still zoomed and buzzed.

After a while, Williams raised his anxious thin face, and looked at the burly rugged Frank opposite, and saw the question in his honest eyes. "It's all right, Frank. I know I like the man, but I'm against crime, and crime alone. This job is ours from crime to conviction — I've not forgotten. Come on man, let's think."

"Good Sir. Well of the I suggest we go and look for joy, in the lad with learning difficulties, Jimmy."

"We could. But we don't know if his trailing after her, was devotion, or fascination of terror. Did he have a sudden brainstorm, and have the strength of insanity that goes with it? Four months ago, were his tears due to grief at his private knowledge of her death, which he was physically unable to tell to any other person? Or were they the whimpering tears of fear, at what he had done, and the terror of being found out. These are the questions, somehow we've got to get answered," Williams pondered.

"So that gives us so far, John Gresham, and Jimmy with learning difficulties."

"For lack of any other leads at the moment, yes Frank. There's her brother, Ashley Wentworth. That's our next line of enquiry. Her friends up there, the London scene, and her brother. We'll have to inform the London Division out of courtesy, even though we don't need them. I've got the smell of this thing now, and would like to complete it ourselves. But while I'm up there, you must continue investigating in Larmer. Well, I'll go and see Canon Pendleton. You know, Frank, what we need at this moment, is that sudden flash that parts the wool."

"Parts the wool, Sir?"

"Yes. I've noticed it sometimes happens. Just where the wool is thickest, and even detective intuition is furred up, a sudden flash from an unexpected quarter will part the wool, and you can see just where to go. We badly need that flash now."

"My experience is, you get there by humdrum surveillance, a lot of slog, and never letting up, Sir. I don't believe in flashes myself," Turner explained.

"No... well, you may be right. I've had them though."

11. The Police visit the Rectory

Canon Pendleton opened the door.

"Ah. Come in Mr Williams. We'd better have our talk in my study, we won't be disturbed there."

Williams could see shadows of anxiety behind the Canon's merry eyes. He sighed a deep tired breath, as he sank into a very comfortable large armchair.

"This is such a wretched business, such an unhappy thing to have happened in my village." There was deep concern in the Canon's a voice as he said 'in my village', almost as if it was 'in my home'. He went on: "you look very tired. You must be working a bit too hard on this. Let me get you a drink. What would you like — whisky?"

"That would do fine, thanks, Canon."

"I'll have one with you," and he left the room to fetch it.

Williams looked about him. The room was quiet and spoke of the background of this man. The walls were hung with team photos of rugby XVs, and rowing VIIIs, with coloured caps hanging on their corners. A rowing oar was fixed to the wall over the door, with the date of the Oxford Boat Race inscribed on it. A large desk contained a jumble of papers. One wall was lined with a floor-to-ceiling bookcase. There were books on philosophy, Macauley's *History of England*, Gibbon's

Decline and Fall of the Roman Empire, and the major English poets. On the mantlepiece was a beautiful marble clock, a vase filled with yellow roses, and a well worn leather-covered Bible. He looked out of the window, at rose beds and trees, behind which the steep grassy downland stretched away.

The Canon returned with the drinks. His sat on a small chair, with his back to the window and faced Williams, who was amused to note how he himself had been placed facing the light — no flies on this man.

"You'll feel better when you've had that." He certainly would. It slid down his throat like satin. The kindness in the Canon's tone was the other thing that Williams needed just now. "I think an investigation into this kind of case would take some time, and can't be solved overnight. My son, Richard, tells me that."

"What does he do?" asked Williams.

"Same as you, he's up at New Scotland Yard, one of the bright boys of the Crime Squad there."

Williams sat bolt upright. "Really? I didn't know."

"Yes. He got a good degree at Oxford, at my old college. He was going to read for the Bar but decided to switch into the Crime Squad instead. And he's never looked back and is a handpicked man now."

"He would be. That's the kind they want."

"He's completely obsessed with it. But you fellows work too hard," the Canon declared.

"Of course! I remember now, I met him from a distance... Detective Superintendent Pendleton. But I never linked him with you, Canon."

"Well no, and I don't suppose you would."

This news revived Williams, almost as much as the Scotch. "If he was brought up in this village, he is the very man I need. Would he know the people here, and what went on?"

"Probably far better than I do," the Canon laughed. "When I finished my ministry in China, and it was time for my children to be educated, we came home to England and here to Lamer Magna. Fortunately, this living was vacant."

"And your son?"

"Richard must have been about nine years old, our eldest child. He knew all the village lads in no time, roamed the country with them, and I'm quite sure learned a lot of poaching off them."

The Canon laughed again. "Richard and I belonged to a shooting syndicate, but I always had the feeling that Richard's tongue was glued very firmly into his cheek, when the beaters put up the birds. Of course, we never openly discussed it. But I wouldn't be surprised if some of the village lads acting as beaters had already got more birds to sell in Bournemouth than we who shot them. It's all part of the country game, you know, great fun!"

"Yes, I've noticed people here seem to have their own rules," said Williams, not quite jokingly.

"Certainly we do. For instance, this term 'permissive society', it makes us smile. It's a fashionable term used in the cities, for something that started here in the country generations ago. I suppose I hardly ever perform a marriage service for a young couple, without the bride having a baby in her tummy first. It's a long-standing country custom."

"And does that apply to other factors in their lives, too?"

"What a specific factor had you in mind?" the Canon enquired.

"The murder of Mrs Amanda Gresham."

The marble clock on the mantelpiece chimed. A hen could be heard in the distance, declaring to the world she had just laid another egg.

Canon Pendleton broke the silence. He said sadly: "I was afraid of that. Poor John. Poor John."

"We've let the Inquest go through with its usual formality. I've not let this conclusion be known yet. I'd rather it wasn't made public, until I've made further investigations."

"Yes. It's quite safe with me," the Canon reassured him.

"But your information about your son at the Yard, is the very flash of light I needed. He can help a great deal with his local knowledge. I have to take the enquiry up to London in any case, Ashley Wentworth, Mrs Amanda Gresham's brother, and others up there, have to be questioned."

"I know Richard will help you all he can."

"You can help us yourself, Canon."

"In any way you ask, Mr Williams."

Williams explained the circumstances surrounding Jimmy, the lad with learning difficulties, and its connection with the case.

"I'll do my best with him, of course," the Canon said, "though I can't guarantee any degree of success. Old Tom, Jimmy's father, was epileptic, it accounts for the poor boy being as he is. Colonel Ferguson knew about it, in fact he often found Old Tom apparently asleep in various parts of the garden. Once he was lying in the drive. He wasn't sleep, but unconsciousness after another fit. He knew, and used to leave him in peace. Sure enough, Old Tom would come around in time, and carry on with his gardening work. He was a skilled gardener, and he and the Colonel had great respect for one another. Funny how they died within a month of each other."

"Well thank you, Canon. You'll have a word with Jimmy in the next day or two, will you?"

"I'll do it in the morning. Can I telephone you anywhere after I've seen him?"

"No, it's better if I come out and have a talk with you about it. Early tomorrow afternoon?"

"Fine. And I'll write to Richard now, then he'll be ready when you get in touch with him."

"Thank you, Canon. That'd be very helpful. I'll see you tomorrow, and thank you for the drink, and for your time."

*   *   *   *   *

Canon Pendleton was waiting for Williams, when he drove up next afternoon. His usually genial face was heavy with seriousness. His eyes and lost their robin brightness. They were not just troubled, but guarded too. Back in the study, Williams asked "What news, Canon?"

The Canon's eyes wavered. "Not very much, I'm afraid, Inspector."

This man's whole manner had altered. The happy, easy, voluble friend of yesterday, had become wary and distant. He continued: "the poor boy is naturally scared, even with me. He shies away, like a frightened foal. He was very fond of Amanda Gresham."

"Fond... or frightened?"

"Fond — like an animal's devotion."

"Mmmm. That doesn't get us very far, does it. Did you get any leads at all, out of him?" asked Williams.

"He did know when she died. That emotional upheaval and weeping four months ago was grief Inspector, not fear."

"Did he appeared to know anything at all in connection with her death?" His question was nicely casual.

The room was very silent. The Canon was thoughtful, as if considering this point. He was looking at his toes. His breathing started to snort through his nostrils. Then he raised his head, and looked Williams squarely in the face.

"If he did, I was unable to understand for certain, what he said. I'm afraid I can't help you, Inspector."

Williams was an expert at gauging people's reactions, when he was not even looking at them. "I see. Well there's no further purpose in wasting your time, Canon." He couldn't keep the disappointment out of his voice.

"Will it be all right to hold the village fete here on Saturday, as planned?"

"Yes, perfectly. But I'd be very glad if you could keep your eyes and ears open, as well. The smallest detail can give us a lead."

"I understand. But you must understand too, that I can't snoop about amongst them. These are my people, and I am their priest and confessor."

"I do understand that, but let us not overlook the principle of justice. A murder has been committed. It's an awkward position for you, isn't it, Canon."

The Canon could see that Williams meant his remark sincerely, whatever way it sounded. He lifted his chin. "It could be, but it won't," he said. "I am not in any way going to allow this case to come between me, and my ministry to this village. They are, and always will be, my first consideration. My work is their happiness, and peace of soul. I'm afraid Inspector, the other must be your work. It is the work you have chosen, I can be no part of it. I want you to understand that."

"I am fully aware of that, Canon. This is not the first time in the experience of the Church, where a choice has to be made between the confessional, and the Courts of Law. Let us understand one another. But thank you for your initial attempt at help." In spite of his disappointment, Williams could do nothing but admire this man. You could trust him anywhere.

As he showed Williams to the door, the Canon brightened up a bit. "I wrote to my son, he'll know all about it by the time you see him."

"Thank you. I'll get in touch with him straightaway. Goodbye."

Williams drove straight back to Salisbury, along the Roman road, which he could see looping over the rolling downs for miles ahead. So, Canon Pendleton had learnt something from Jimmy after all. Something that had had a disturbing effect on him, too disturbing to divulge. After all, every member of that darned village, rich or poor, were members of his flock.

*   *   *   *   *

Williams fumed into headquarters. "Send Sergeant Turner to me," he called to the constable at the desk. He strode into his office, throwing his hat onto the hat stand. He paced the room, his face deeply grooved with frustrated anger.

Solid Frank Tanner quietly entered the room and took a look at his superior. "No joy at Larmer Rectory, Sir?"

"Joy!" Williams exploded. "You must be joking, Frank. But that merry Canon knows something from crazy Jimmy in the village, and what's more, he's not telling. Okay, so that village community is having us all on, from Constable Cope, to Jimmy, to the Rector, and probably to the MP Mr Gresham himself."

"They've all seen a threat to their clan, Sir, so they've closed ranks behind a barrier of silence."

"You're dead right, Frank. And one gets the feeling in the shop, in that pub, and even as you walk up the street between those cottages, that the whole damn place is watching your every step. And they're murmuring too, but not within earshot. Well, I'm off to London by the next train. And guess what! The Canon's son, Richard Pendleton, is Detective Superintendent Pendleton of the Yard."

Frank Turner let out a soft whistle. "That's a bit of luck, Sir!"

"Let's hope he is more helpful than his father. Anyhow, I'm off to see him, he'd better live up to his reputation That's all." Bitterness rasped through his voice.

"If I could add a personal word of warning, Sir."

"Add what you damn well like."

"Don't overlook promotion. Maybe it'll be his job you're offered next, when he's budged up another rung. If you criticise his father, in your present mood, you may not be offered it," Turner bravely suggested.

Williams laughed for the first time. "You do me good, Frank. I'll be tactful, don't worry."

"It could be the flash you're looking for."

"It had better be. Meanwhile Frank, keep going at Larmer. See if you can squeeze a bit more out of Cope. Be in and out of the pub. See if you can get them talking about anything at all, even the crops. Always be there, every time they look over their shoulders. Strike up an acquaintance with the publican, they know most things that go on."

"Oh, I've been doing that already, Sir. The original man at the pub died about a year ago. He was a retired groom, and his wife baked the village bread, in one of the old baker's ovens, situated in that side cottage, adjacent to the pub. The new chap is an ex-RAF type, with a handlebar moustache, very outgoing and talkative. He's trying to build up the pub into a roadhouse, cold suppers with salmon, duck, and that. He wants to turn it into an evening run-out from all those seaside resorts, round about."

"Does he now! The village won't like that."

"They don't. They hate his guts. But this chap's made a modern cosy bar, in the part where the baker's oven used to be. He's opened up the oven, and decorated it with hidden lighting, and a big bowl of flowers. There are copper warming pans, horse brasses, kettles, and red shaded lights and things. It looks attractive, he'll make a good job of it in time. He's kept the Snug part of the pub just the same, brown paint and all, for the use of the village."

"You've not been wasting your time, have you." Williams was impressed.

"Thank you, Sir. Mind you, the hate is mutual, he can't stand the village folk, refers to them as 'Yokels'."

"What's his name?"

"Wing Commander Cowper."

"There you are, you see. His name is down on Cope's dossier, but just name and occupation. Not a word about this relationship with the people. You got the lot, and you don't even bloody well live there. Frank, we've got to ginger up Cope a bit. But stick around yourself, get friendly with the Wing-Co. He may be a useful man to us, especially as he is not part of the Club."

"I reckon we've got to solve this case on our own, and rely on nobody else, not even Cope."

"The thing that bothers me, Frank, is the way all these village characters appear to be prototypes. People just aren't like that, they're more complex, more mixed up. So who's fooling who?"

"So long as you're aware of that, Sir, I don't think you need to worry. It'd take a wily bird to fool you."

"They're all bloody poachers, and wilier than the birds. I'll leave you to the Larmer scene, you're welcome to it. I'll go up and tackle the London end."

12. <u>Williams and Richard Pendleton visit Ashley Wentworth</u>

As Detective Superintendent Pendleton of Scotland Yard studied Williams' report of the case, Williams watched his face. Yes, he had his mother's serene grey eyes, but his build was his father's — medium height, with those square rugby shoulders. He had the same regular classic features as his mother, he was even smiling her quiet smile, as he read the report. It had not been written for his amusement. He looked up when he had finished, and caught the criticism in Williams' eyes.

"Thank you. This is a lucid, well-constructed report. It brought back to me the whole atmosphere of Larmer as I read it. It's a world on its own."

"So I've discovered Sir," Williams replied.

"I don't expect you found my father too helpful, reading between the lines of your report."

Watch it, Frank had said!

"I think he'd like to have been, but he is in a difficult position," Williams told Richard after a pause.

"He would sincerely want to help, you know. But every member of the village is like a member of his own family. He grieves with their griefs, triumphs with their successes, bolsters them up in their disappointments, and tears them off a right good strip if they behave badly. As a boy, I used to wonder which he loved most, us or the villagers. He loves each one of them, and they trade on it, turn to him with every petty bother, as if they were still children, and his children at that. He never missed his own family growing up and leaving too much, he's got all these other children in the village. He's a great person."

Richard Pendleton walked to the window. He stood looking down at Victoria Embankment. He didn't see the red London buses, traffic pressed together in an untidy mess, or motorboats on the Thames. He saw a valley tucked away among high downland slopes, and bridle paths of white chalk leading to the silent woods. He saw charming white cottages, gardens blooming with flowers which told you the seasons. He saw some of the farming faces he had known so well, striding up the downland slopes, driving cattle up the valley pastures. There, these faces possessed confidence and authority, nowhere else.

He turned back to Williams. "I shouldn't wonder if you've come up against a conspiracy of silence, Inspector."

"That's exactly right, even to the village constable."

"Yes. I can see we are going to have a bit of a job here."

"We... Sir?"

"Yes, if you don't mind the Yard butting in, I'll go along with you." He did not miss the expression on Williams' face. He explained, "I have a deep affection for Larmer, but you won't find me following my father's example. Crime is crime, and crime begets crime. And that's my job, as much as it's yours."

William face cleared as he heard this, which was given in a clear authoritative tone. "Our first investigation should be Ashley Wentworth, Mrs Gresham's brother."

"Yes, Sir. I thought that too."

"I can tell you a bit about him. A couple of years ago, he was arrested and remanded on bail by the Drug Squad. He was subsequently convicted and fined. It was cannabis and LSD. At the time, hard drugs were not his scene. I remember the case very clearly, because he was Amanda Gresham's brother."

"Since then Sir?"

"He's been lying pretty low. He is a strange fellow, in his mid-30s, yet his friends all seem to be kids of 20, or early 30s, except for one of them, a chap called Arnold Braithwaite. We still keep some surveillance on the place."

"So, an immature character?"

"Very probably in many ways. And one who craves admiration. His sort only get that from the youngster hippie generation."

"How often did he go down to Larmer?" enquired Williams.

"About two or three times a year. He always made his visits when John Gresham was out of the way, in London, or was at The House as an MP. He would take a gaggle of friends down there with him, the whole place went wild. It filled the village with boggle-eyed scandal for months."

"Went wild? In what way, Sir?"

"They used to dress up in crinolines, velvet breeches, and highwayman's outfits, and so on. One wonders where they got all the gear from. They used to romp all over the grounds, and 'Coo-ee' to each other through the trees. They were pretty high all the time. At night, it turned into an orgy, whether it was on drugs, or alcohol, I just don't know, but I suspect it was drugs. Young Constable Cope used to keep well out of the way, while that lark was going on."

"But John Gresham must have got to hear of it on his return."

"He knew all right. He turned a blind eye to a lot of things he knew, for her sake. You see, his life was devoted to keeping her calm, on an even keel. To object to anything, would have been to rouse her into one of her fury episodes."

"Did they have servants?" enquired Williams.

"Only the housekeeper, Mrs Clark, and she adored Amanda, the only person that did. Mrs Clark would never complain. But I've heard rumours that Arnold

Braithwaite, one of Ashley Wentworth's young friends, was also a boyfriend of Amanda Gresham."

"Really? I think we should pursue this Arnold Braithwaite."

"We will. But before we interview Braithwaite, we'll pay a call on Ashley Wentworth, at his home in Cadogan Square. He should just be getting up about now, 11 am. He is a wealthy over-indulgent character who's never done a stroke of work in his life."

*   *   *   *   *

The door was opened by Ashley Wentworth himself. Richard greeted him, and asked to come in. Williams noted Wentworth's fat pink face, receding ginger hair, and expressiveness watery blue eyes. Wentworth led them into a large room, with gilt encrusted furniture, rich satin curtains, a thick crimson carpet, and a glinting chandelier above them.

"You'd better tell me what's on your mind," Wentworth said acidly to Richard Pendleton, through a forced smile. He completely ignored Williams, as they sat down on brocade regency chairs.

"This is a terrible business about Amanda, isn't it," said Richard, playing it cool.

"It's worse than that! John has a great deal to answer for — I'm not at all satisfied. He should have taken greater care of her. He was her male nurse for enough years, wasn't he?"

"When did you last see her?"

"Let me see... It was before I went away. I know I was away when she was found missing."

"Where were you?"

"Bermuda."

"What date did you return to this country?" asked Richard.

"Good Heavens man! You don't expect me to remember that, do you? I know I came back as soon as I got the news that she was missing. I went straight down to Larmer and told that virtuous John a few things for his health."

"When did you last see her alive?"

"I've told you, before I went away. She was staying up here in her Mayfair apartment. We had a bit of a party here."

"Apart from your friends, were any of her own friends at the party?"

"I imagine so, I can't really remember. Dammit Richard, it was some months ago."

Richard got up and stood looking into Cadogan Square. The room was so silent. Richard swung round suddenly. "Would her friend Arnold Braithwaite have been among your guests?"

"That's typical, isn't it! Your drug chaps picked him up, when they picked me up, didn't they! You knew he was her boyfriend, so now you're after him. That means the poor bugger hasn't a chance, with the so-called Justice of this country."

His bluster made no impression on Richard who said: "Arnold Braithwaite was basically poor, but strangely only in patches. He was unemployed, with no personal money except what Amanda gave him. Of course, he got a little money from being a pusher."

"You've no evidence of that," Ashley Wentworth broke in quickly.

"No. Only the knowledge that's why he hasn't been arrested yet. But at the moment, I'm not concerned about his drug activities. It's his money sources I find interesting — in between he had periods of extreme wealth and luxurious living. His activities as a pusher, would never have made that kind of money, but something else has. After this living it up, back he would go to a period of being broke. According to Amanda Gresham's bank statement, it was while he was broke that she supplied him with money. But what was the source that supplied him with this top level living, in between? It wasn't drugs, so it was something else."

Ashley Wentworth's protruding eyes lost their deadness and looked startled. Richard saw it.

Richard said with a carefully judged rap of impatience: "I expect it's news to you that Braithwaite went down to Larmer, and stayed there for three days with Amanda while John was in session in The House as an MP. He left suddenly, after they had had a violent row."

"She was always having rows with everyone, all her life. It was one of her habits, she thrived on it. I suppose you even know what the row was about..." and yet there was a trace of fear behind Ashley Wentworth's dry tone.

Richard looked at him with a dead pan expression. "I have my ideas, quite apart from guessing that money was involved."

Wentworth looked uneasy. He switched on a crooked smile and faced Richard. "How the hell do you know all this?"

"I have my sources," was all Richard would tell him. "Arnold Braithwaite left Larmer Manor the day before Amanda disappeared, and only a few hours before John's unexpected return from London. We need to see Braithwaite, where does he live?"

"At the moment I don't know. He's sleeping around at various friends pads, couch surfing. He hasn't got a settled address yet. He stays here quite a bit, but he's not here at the moment."

"He's never been on the humdrum mill of work, has he?"

"Give the fellow a chance. He was to have worked in the family firm, but he was a bit tactless with his stodgy family. Stupid of him, after all he couldn't afford to be, when they were loaded with all their money — damn nearly millionaires. They threw him out, when he was used to living a great life, with plenty of cash behind him. That happened years ago, and Amanda's affair with him, kept him going all these years. It's ironic, when you realise that when John marries again, his new wife will be the one to benefit from Amanda's money."

"Who says that John intends to marry again?" said Richard angrily. Something in the other man's tone, had flicked him on the raw.

Wentworth rolled his eyes at Richard. "No one. Purely guesswork, old boy, purely guesswork."

"What happens to the money if John dies?" Richard asked.

"Ah! I was wondering when you would come around to that. It all comes to me, dear boy," Wentworth tried to produce another smile.

"Look Richard," said Wentworth. "I didn't kill Amanda, and at present I haven't any plans on killing John — not for these reasons anyway."

The door opened quietly, and in came a young man with perfectly dressed long wavy hair, and fringes swinging from the edge of his leather jacket. He wore rows of beads.

"Coffee anyone?" he asked archly.

"Oh, thank you Colin. Do get some, there's a love." Wentworth smiled gently at the boy.

Richard had always guessed that this was the scene. He said firmly: "I'm prepared to strike a bargain with you. You must arrange for Arnold Braithwaite to be here tomorrow morning at 11 o'clock, and I will see to it that your parties are not raided. You know don't you, that next time the Drug Squad would remand you in custody, and if convicted, you'd be sent to prison."

Wentworth's pink face turned a dusky mauve. "You're not giving me much time. Suppose I can't find him?"

"If you can't, the police will. Please tell your friend that we don't need coffee. We'll show ourselves out."

*   *   *   *   *

After they had walked around the corner, Richard's face relaxed. "That's the only way to handle him, by being firm. Come on, let's have some coffee ourselves, and a talk."

Over their coffees Richard continued, "it's important that Ashley should remain at large for a bit, to lead us to Amanda's friends, Arnold Braithwaite in particular."

"Do you think Wentworth was involved in the murder?"

"Not for a minute. But the kind of fear that his corrupt cocky type possesses may lead us to the man who is."

Williams said slowly: "You see, when Braithwaite left Amanda in a rage, he may have stayed around Larmer all night. He may have been sleeping rough somewhere, especially if he'd been trying to squeeze money out of her — that's possible. He couldn't go openly back to the house, once her husband had returned."

"I think round there, someone would have seen him hanging about."

"That's another line of enquiry, to be made at Larmer," said Williams.

"If he was there, they'd have seen him all right. Those woods are pretty well alive at night. I know. As a kid I used to poach there, along with the village lads. My father never knew," he laughed.

"Oh, but he did, Sir. He had a pretty good idea. Anyhow, he told me so," Williams was laughing too.

"The Foxy old so-and-so. And he never gave a hint of it! Not much moves down there, but some keen country eye spots it, especially if it's someone foreign to the landscape." They were both silent for a while, before Richard said "what d'you think yourself? Does the murderer come from up here, or from Larmer? Before you were posted down to Salisbury, you were known for your detection intuitiveness, I had heard of you."

"I've got my own ideas, Sir, but it's better not to tell you them just yet. I don't want to influence your own conclusions, I need your open mind."

Richard turned to Williams. "You're right. I have a theory about Arnold Braithwaite but nothing definite yet. More evidence is what we need now. Braithwaite has been away from London the last few months. If we can get him back, he should give us the evidence. I'll arrange for surveillance on Ashley Wentworth, who is a slippery customer."

Williams knew better than to prod a superior in to explaining more fully. He had to look pleasant, and to wait.

13. <u>The prime lead for the police slips away</u>

As soon as the door closed behind the two detectives, Ashley Wentworth moved surprisingly quickly for such a portly man. He sped across the hall, calling to the boy Colin that he'd be back soon, and to answer no bells. He then went out to his grey Bentley, parked outside.

He nervously picked at a rough bit of cuticle round his thumbnail as he drove, glaring at traffic lights every time they held him up. It seems his life depended on green-go lights.

He reached Eaton Place and walked to a large imposing house, converted into apartments. He leaped up the steps to the porticoed front door and rang the bell of the ground floor apartment. While he waited, he looked anxiously up and down the quiet street, but the only person to be seen was an elderly lady taking her poodle for a walk. At last the door was opened.

"Arnold here?" Ashley asked.

"I'll say," the man answered. "Got a hell of a cold turkey, the worst I've seen. He's laid out in bed with it."

Ashley slipped inside. "Take me to him".

The man took him through the luxurious apartment to a small unfurnished back room. It was dimly lit by a small window, looking onto the backs of other houses. There was a thin mat on the floor, beside a divan bed against the wall. Peering out from under a rumpled heap of blankets, was the grey glistening face of a man. His eyes were like deep holes, and his hair was matted with sweat, his teeth chattering through his hanging lips.

As Ashley went towards him, the man's pale hand reached out for a vomit bowl beside the bed. His retching could be heard down the passage. At last, he fell back against his pillow, wrung out with exhaustion. Ashley saw Arnold Braithwaite's wrist and hand lying inert on the blanket, then it started to tremble. Soon his whole body was trembling under the blankets, and his teeth chattering.

"God, Arnold! What are you hooked on?"

"Horse," he gasped. "Skin popping. No fix for three days. For Christ's sake... get me some... Ashley."

"You look really shitty."

The shaking began to pass. "Man, I feel it. Puking fit to die."

"You silly sod! Why the hell didn't you stick to cannabis, like the rest of us? You know the score with the hard stuff!"

"There was nothing to worry about at the start — only shot half a jack at a time."

"When did you get hooked on it?"

"About four months ago."

"After Amanda went missing?" asked Ashley.

"Yup! Got all hung up... I'm going to puke!"

Arnold grabbed for the bowl, and Ashley turned away. The sound of gut retching made his own stomach heave. Soon, it was back to the sound of chattering teeth, and shallow breathing. Ashley turned back to the curled up, cowering figure in bed. He was so thin. Ashley waited until the spasm was over, he saw the needle marks on his wasted arms, some of which looked a bit infected. To think, this was once the man that the girls all fell for, and until four months ago, an elegant 'man about town' who was invited to smart parties and black tie dinners.

When the spasm had passed, Arnold could only gasp "get us a fix. God, man! Don't just stand there — get me a fix. Only one will put me right."

"I can't get you heroin, but here's a smoke of cannabis." Ashley lit it for him, and put it between his lips. "It won't give you a buzz like H of course, but it'll help your turkey a bit, for a minute." Ashley waited for the smoke to work, then he said: "Look Arnold, there is nothing cool about a junkie. We both know that. He is just a zombie, an ancient body with a young voice."

"Yuh! It's sussed me right out."

"Okay, so you know it's a drastic thing to do. Amanda knew it was drastic, that's why she always stuck to cannabis, and acid. You were all right on it, we all were, it gave you a high enough kick. So why get hooked on this bloody hard stuff?"

"I'm not as calculating as you Wentworths. And I needed escape. I take off. It lets me out."

"Lets you out of what, Arnold?"

"Amanda partly. Without her... the world's fallen in on me. I wanted her before she even knew Gresham... she wouldn't have me. I could have worked then, could have worked for her, but she needed some kind of anchor, while she played around with me."

"But you wouldn't have stayed together! You'd have killed each other," said Ashley.

"Yuh! We did anyhow. We'd have had fun first though."

"But you had plenty of that in any case. God, that last time at my pad — I had to go in and shut you both up at four in the morning. There you were in bed, both screaming with laughter, like a couple of crazy cats. I was bothered that the neighbours would complain, and then the Fuzz would push their noses in again. Yeah! You two had lots of fun for years. You'd never have had that, if she'd married you. Anyhow, you hadn't enough money in those days."

"I'd have worked. I could then, in the family firm manufacturing shoes. Jesus, shoes! She'd have trampled all over me, in our own bloody shoes. Anyway, she'd got plenty of dough herself."

"Arnold, what happened at Larmer? You went down to see her there, after your week at my place. It was just before she disappeared, and you went alone. Why? What happened?"

"I don't want to talk about it, or remember."

"You've got to, Arnold. You're in dead trouble, boy! I've got to scoop you out of it."

"Why bother! The game's pretty nearly up."

"Amanda would laugh her head off at you, if she could hear you! The game's never up you halfwit! If you throw the sponge in now, you will go in for our long stretch. Think of the boredom, not to mention the food!"

"I can't remember much. We got the highest ever at your pad all that week, not cannabis, just plain sex. We didn't need anything else. It was marvellous! Then she suddenly switched on this going-home bit, the way she did sometimes. I couldn't go on grooving around here without her, and business was slack, and there were things I needed to know. So, I drove down to fetch her back in my new car, the one I bought with the profits... from the recent business deal. On the day we were going to drive back, we had a terrific row — it put all other rows in the shade."

"What was it about?"

"Can't remember."

"Oh yes you can! Cash, was it? Were you putting in for a rise? Or did she catch you in the act of operating one of your business deals? Were you heisting her with her own petard?" asked Ashley.

"Can't remember. Anyhow, she threw me out."

"Then what did you do?"

"I just drove about a bit. Thought I'd go back and see her later on, when she'd calmed down. Then I saw Gresham driving up the village, back from London. That was a near one. They didn't expect him back for some days. I couldn't go back to her then."

"What made him come back so unexpectedly? Had he heard you were there perhaps, or learnt about your business deals? Look, if I'm to help you, you've got to come clean with me." Ashley was firm.

"I'm telling you what I know. And I don't know what brought the bugger back."

"Where did you spend the night?"

"In the car, somewhere on the Downs. I'd been walking, seemed for miles — not used to that sort of thing. I dropped in at a pub for some grub."

"Then what?"

"Went back to the car, drove to some spot, so tired, I'd had a few in the pub, I just dropped off. Remember waking with a hell of a fright, a cow mooing through the car window beside me. Made a split for London."

"Where did you stay when you got up here?"

"Let myself into your pad. You were still away. It felt bloody empty without her. Got so depressed, I found this pusher, and got some H of him. I needed a bigger kick than cannabis." Arnold looked as if he had more to say, and wasn't able to say it.

Ashley waited but the room was silent now. Then he said slowly "if all of this is true... then you've got no alibi of your movements, after you left Amanda."

This appeared to mean nothing to Arnold.

Ashley continued: "and that was your first fix of heroin?"

"Yuh! Thought I'd try it once and then leave it — let it turn me on, while I got over the turgid bit. But H... you just can't try it once, and leave it."

Arnold suddenly flung back the bedclothes, pouring with sweat, his trembling limbs glistening. He closed his eyes, spent from this maximum effort. The stench from the exposed bed, made Ashley step back towards the door. He had seen some grisly sights in his life, but this one took the Oscar.

From the open door he said, "Arnold, did anyone see you around Larmer, that night or next morning?"

"Can't remember," he gasped. "Can't... remember."

"Can you stand?"

He shook his head. "Can't even get to the loo. That's why they put me in this cave."

"I'll get you help," said Ashley.

"Man, just get me a fix!" He pulled the bed clothes back, shivering again now. "Going to puke," he growled, fumbling for the bowl. Ashley opened his wallet and put three £20 notes beside the bed.

"I'll get help," he said again, then quietly left the room. He saw the other man, hovering in the hall. "Can I use your phone?"

He went to the phone in the hall and dialled his own number. "Colin, now listen carefully, Ashley here. Pack a suitcase for yourself, and one for me. I've decided we will leave, to winter in the sun. Pack what you think we will need, but don't forget passports, or the wallet in my briefcase, you know the one I mean. Call a taxi, I'll meet you at Heathrow Airport, Terminal 3, by the Swiss Air weigh-in, in about half an hour. If you don't see me there, just wait till I arrive. Don't mess about, we've got to get off before the Fuzz trail us. Oh, and don't forget to lock up, and put the burglar alarm on. See you at Heathrow, I'll explain when we meet. Bye, now."

Ashley turned to the other man. "I had meant to take our friend here with me, but he is too ill to move."

"He can't even stand. That's why I put him in the room kept for turkeys. Silly bugger, messing things up."

"I must call the doctor at the Treatment Centre, he's got to have medical care, or he will die. He is very sick indeed. The doctor may come during the day, so you'd better get cracking clearing up any evidence. You better warn the rest of the bunch to keep away, they're sure to put a watch on this place. And you'd better hide away anything else you'd rather they didn't see."

"They'll find nothing."

"He tells me he's been turned on H for the last four months."

"Yup."

"Then the last four months must have run your business down a bit."

"I have other sources, he is not the only one. He is pretty skint himself now — I'm bloody keeping him!"

"Yeah! Looks as if you'll have to for a while," Ashley replied.

As the front door closed behind him, Ashley looked up and down the street. A taxi rounded the corner, and drew up outside a house lower down. A woman with a shopping basket got out, paid the driver, and disappeared into the house. A black cat stretched and yawned in the sun, on the porch next door. Someone closed an upstairs window in a house opposite. He could see his grey Bentley parked at the far end of the street, with not a soul watching from any doorway.

He walked to his car, and drove quickly away, first to his bank, then out to the airport... and no car had followed him.

*   *   *   *   *

That evening, an apprehensive sergeant faced Richard Pendleton in his Scotland Yard office. "I sent a man round to Cadogan Square as soon as I could get hold of one — it would be about half an hour after the you phoned, Sir. It must have been all of an hour all told, by the time he got there, he got stuck in a traffic jam in Knightsbridge."

"And they had gone by then?" barked Richard.

"They must have. There's been no movement all day or evening. No lights. He tried the doors and windows, there are locked, and a burglar-proof screen. Not a sign of a soul about, Sir."

"Did he ask around?"

"Yes, Sir. The housekeeper next door said she saw the boy leave in a taxi, with two suitcases, about midday."

"And the Bentleys gone?"

"Yes Sir. It has been traced to a multi-storey car park at Heathrow Airport. That's all we know at present. I've got a man there, checking the flight passenger lists."

"Hmmm," snarled Richard. "I'll bet he is off to Geneva to pick up some money from his Swiss bank account, and then off somewhere in the big wide world. So, he's slipped through our fingers."

"Shall I leave the constable on duty in Cadogan Square, Sir?"

"No, take him off. There's no point now." Richard looked across at the listening Williams, then got up paced round the office.

Williams quiet tone broke through his bitterness. "A determined man can always slip away, Sir." He waited until he knew he had Richard's full attention, and then said: "I think our next visit should be to Marion Ferguson, if you agree, Sir."

Everything about Richard suddenly became immobile. "There'll be nothing to learn from that quarter," he said quietly. "She hasn't been near Beech Farm for two years."

"How do you know, Sir?"

"We do know. It was locked up solidly, and only the estate agent had the keys until it was sold. It was I who handed them to the agents, on her behalf."

"But there was nothing to stop her keeping a key back — it wouldn't have been the first time that had happened."

"I've known her very well, all our life in fact. It would break her heart to go back, it very nearly did to leave. Anyhow, crime could never have been part of her makeup, she isn't that way."

"You can never tell that. People do unlikely things when pushed beyond a limit."

"Not this girl, Inspector. Even if she had retained a key, and revisited Beech Farm, she could never have done so without the whole village knowing."

"But why? She may not have put any lights on at night, if she didn't want her visit to be known about."

Richard laughed. "My dear fellow, she only had to be in the house, and someone would have spotted movement behind the windows. No one can escape Larmer vigilance, particularly if an empty house is involved, and belonging to their beloved Miss Marion. It wouldn't surprise me if they hadn't organised a rota of watchers among themselves, to safeguard her property." It was a statement, yet underneath there were echoes...

"You could be right. The new owners said there was no sign of the usual vandalism to property that has been unoccupied for some time. They told me someone even kept the grass cut, on the banks and the lawns, and the box hedge clipped, and even the clippings burnt on a bonfire."

"What did I tell you! I'm not in the least surprised. I know Larmer pretty well." He laughed again.

"But all the same, I think it'd be worth a visit to her, Sir. She might drop out some small detail that would lead us to an important clue. It's often the apparently small unimportant bit that is the key to the whole picture."

"I think it would only cause her unnecessary distress. She had enough over her father's death, and leaving Larmer. She couldn't be involved in this crime, it's physically impossible for her to have pushed Amanda Gresham down the well, she was such a light little thing."

He got up, walked across the room to the window, and stood silently looking out of it. Yes, such a little thing. He remembered the day that they had sat on the grassy side of a Down that fell steeply into a narrow valley, and then rose on the other side to a closely wooded copse. The whole ground was spongey with rabbit warrens, the fine grass nibbled merely bald, and white-tailed rabbits scudding around. They sat in the sun, calling out every name they knew, and listening to the echo flung back at them, followed by higher and fainter echoes in the hills.

"Oh, isn't this fun," she had whispered excitedly. They listened open mouthed as they heard "this fun, this fun," hissing round the trees and over the hills.

Then suddenly she had leaped crying: "Oh Richard, things are crawling all over me, and stinging."

"Stinging... stinging... stinging..." came back at them from the hill opposite. Then he saw the ant's nest that she had been sitting on. He had picked her up, put her over his shoulder, and ran all the way home to the Rectory. He had seen his mother's astonished face, as she saw him leap up the stairs, with Marion screaming over his shoulder, and plonked her straight into a cold bath. She must have been about thirteen then.

And the next winter they had ridden over on their bikes, to join the New Forest Beagles. He was in his first year at Oxford then. His parents told him to look after her, as she was still a schoolgirl. She had run well, and kept up, until they had to cross a bog. There she kept dithering on the edge, while the Huntsman and the field ran past her. He could see her now, with her short fair curly hair windblown, her cheeks pink in the cold air.

He had picked her up then too, and run across the bog, the mud squelching over his shoes. He caught up with the rest of the field, and then set her down. She'd always felt and looked like a little fairy. And later, when she was seventeen, her parents allowed him to take her to an Oxford Ball at his college. She had worn a lovely white gown which took his breath away. The whole evening had passed in a dream.

"Though Amanda was slim, she'd have made two of Marion," he said at last, as if from a great distance.

"Are you married, Sir?"

"No, but what's that got to do with it?" Richard asked.

"Nothing really. It's just that, like myself, it leaves you freer to follow investigations, at any hour you want."

Williams had a sideways view of this man dreaming out of the window. At that moment, everything about him looked clenched, his hands, his jaws, his eyes. So that was it!

Richard returned to his desk and sat down. He said wearily, "it would be a happier thing for her, if you could see your way ahead, without having to question Marion Ferguson."

"But surely, Sir, all this distress after her father dying, and having to leave Larmer, was two whole years ago. She'd have got over all that quite a bit by now, surely, especially as she is still young. She's probably got involved in her Nottingham life by now. You probably think it's worse for her, than it really is," he persisted.

"You must do exactly what you think fit, Inspector." It was the formal rather rigid tone, of a superior officer.

"You mean... you're not going on with this enquiry with me?"

"No, I think it best not to. I've got a lot of other cases on my hands up here."

"But…" Williams said.

"I've helped you as far as I'm able at the moment at the London end. Though I would like you to stay here for a day or two, in case we get Arnold Braithwaite run to ground, then you will have more of the picture. But this is your case. I'm sure it would be best that you should complete it yourself. I'm here for you to refer to anytime you need me, and whenever I can help you, I shall be glad to do so. You're very competent, and I'm sure you'd rather complete this case of your own, in your own way, without The Yard butting in."

"I see," said Williams thoughtfully.

"I'm afraid the London end has not been much help to you, except to fill in a few background details."

"It's done that very clearly, thank you, Sir. Local knowledge is one of the biggest helps." The dryness of his tone matched that of Richard's.

"I could get Ashley Wentworth found, and brought home again, if you really need him. I stress 'really', as it's an expensive operation."

"I'll let you know if I feel it's necessary, Sir. At present, I don't think it is."

"Why?"

"I've got a very strong feeling, that it's someone more closely connected with Larmer than Ashley Wentworth."

"He's run away, don't forget."

"That might be from a drug scare, and not a murder scare."

14. <u>Kate and David hear strange things at the village fete</u>

"Oh David! What shall I wear for this dreary fete thing?" Kate asked.

"Sweetie! You sound as if it's a funeral you're getting dressed for, not a village fete!"

"I feel as if it is. The hell is, the person who did this murder could be there, and I could even be bloody talking to him, and not know."

"Don't think like that, Darling. It'll be all right, and I'll be with you, and it's a glorious afternoon. Cheer up! Now let's see what you can dosh yourself up in. Whatever else you do, don't wear one of your revealing necklines. Put on something fairly demure."

She laughed at that. "If I went trolling around looking demure, it'd be at a discount. Not my scene."

"Right, it's not. Well, dosh up something simple. That's your style." He dodged the cushion that she threw at him. "But hurry, darling. We're late and as it is," he said.

They arrived at the Rectory Garden just as the brass band were erecting music stands, and shuffling chairs around. One or two of them, were burping some limbering notes down their instruments. As Kate went into the marquee, she could see the trestle tables lining three sides of it, already piled with goods. Mrs Marsh was presiding over a stall of home-made cakes, jams, lardy bread, and bottled fruit and pickles. She had the look on her face that at least she knew how to sell her stall, even if the amateurs all around, hadn't got a clue.

Kate recognised the gardener from the Manor, who was in charge of the home produce stall. It was bristling with runner beans, bunches of crisp carrots, and lettuces. Enormous marrows were piled up in layers. She watched a very old man hobble up to the stall on his stick, his face shrivelled and wrinkled like the skin of a dried apricot. He handed in a basket of summer cabbages.

"They be a bumper craarrp this year," he croaked. "It be that tharr pig manure Joe gave I".

The flower stall, her particular chore, was stretched across one end of the marquee, with brilliant splurges of blossom, overlapping the white elephant stall next to it. Mrs Bennett was busily arranging armfuls of roses in big jugs.

"Ah, there you are at last Kate," she said in her fussy managing way, as soon as she clapped eyes on her. "Will you divide all those sweet peas into bunches of twelve, put them in these pots, and put these price tickets against them. Then there are the dahlias to bunch too." There was no doubt who was managing the flower stall. Jane Lloyd put her head through sheaves of greenery and gladiolas, to call "Hi!" to her, and then gave her a quick wink, after a quick glance at Mrs Bennett. They both laughed. "Now come on girls, don't hang around," Mrs Bennet said. "We're not nearly ready, and the fete's due to be opened at any moment." She was used to obedience from people, as well as from her horses.

Kate couldn't help feeling slightly giggly, as she saw the Doctor and Mrs Macdonald stagger backwards and forwards with their huge pots of precious chrysanthemums, with flower heads like un-used mops. There was a smell of damp grass, mingling with the flower perfumes, and the sun warmed trees outside.

It was a relief to see Mrs Pendleton moving from stall to stall, admiring the helper's efforts, her serene smile smoothing away the rivalries and irritations. Kate waved to her from beneath swathes of dahlias. She immediately came to her side.

"Dear girl," she said. "I don't know which is the prettier, the flowers, or the girl arranging them".

"You are nice. That's just what I needed to straighten me up. This really isn't my scene, you know."

"You don't know the half of it yet. The brass band hasn't even started." When Kate laughed, Mrs Pendleton's grey eyes looked satisfied. "You're helping me to serve teas later on, isn't she Mrs Bennett!" The firmness in Mrs Pendleton's voice, prevented any objection from Mrs Bennett.

"Just let me know," Kate said happily. "By the way, have you seen how David's getting on?"

"Yes, he and John Gresham are making a great job of erecting sacking to catch the balls round Aunt Sally. Judging by the seriousness of their consultations, it's going to be a structure to last for all time!" She laughed as she moved on.

Kate saw the garden gradually become crowded with people, arriving from all the surrounding villages. The air was thick with the burr of Dorset/Wiltshire brogue. There seemed to be far more chatter than usual from these country folk. She had come to regard them as pretty inarticulate, as if threatened by something.

The downland hills were looking down on this small community. The larks sang into a clear sky. Ripe wheat was swaying in the surrounding fields. This season was marching on, and if clouds were gathering over the village, it seemed not to mind.

The Canon's laugh and jovial welcome, could be heard all over the Rectory grounds, as he helped with the archery contest. But as she talked to him Kate could see shadows of anxiety behind his beaming face. It seemed as if he looked around his village family, with an even deeper affection, and concern. They had become still more his children, as he felt them turn to him for reassurance. She wondered if they ever realised how lucky they were.

The pigeons were cooing contentedly from the trees. A lick of gold was beginning to colour their leaves. Soon the harvest would be gathered in. Later, while she helped to put out trays of sandwiches on garden tables, alongside piles of cups and plates, she could hear the brass band blowing its resounding way through the 'Merry Widow'. Her mouth twitched in and out of a smile, as she noticed all the cows in a nearby field, had stopped grazing in surprise. They huddled together, and looked mournfully round towards the Rectory, their swishing tails flicking flies off their backs. Then slowly, their curiosity won, and they lolloped across to the fence separating them from the rectory garden. By the time the band was in mid-blow through Madame Butterfly, the leading cow pealed out the most mournful *Moooo* of her maternal career, and was then joined by almost every other member of the herd.

Kate could hardly believe it. The bandmaster evidently recognised that the competition was too great and brought an abrupt end to Madam Butterfly. Then the men shook the spittle out of their instruments, while some laughed, and said "them Cows!"

Kate thought this was just like a stage farce of country life, that made West End theatre audiences laugh. And yet here it was all for real, even to the corpse of the Squire's Lady down the well. Could the answer for continuing to live at Beech Farm, be found in treating the whole thing has a joke? Really? Yes but, murder was scarcely joke material!

"Kate!" The Canon broke in on her thoughts. "Come and meet the oldest inhabitant of the village. The oldest member, and the newest!" he introduced them gaily.

"'Ow be Ma'am," old Mr Whitt wheezed, touching his cap.

The leather furrows on his face looked grained with weather, and crops, and livestock. His speech was slow, but Kate got the idea that his keen old eyes missed nothing. It was a sure bet that he could smell through snow to where lambs were buried.

"It's nice to meet you. We're gradually getting to know the village. We're the newcomers at Beech Farm."

"Yuss. I 'earred on it. It be nice up tharr, it be."

She looks at his bent figure, and gnarled hands, leaning on two sticks. "Are you keeping well?" she asked.

"No, I be proper poorly. Got a cold, see. Never knew it be that, until Sunday service. The Canon 'ere'll tell yer, they played that tharr 'fight the good fight', so o' courrse I closes my eyes, and throws back me 'ead to 'oller, and no sound do come. I know then I'd got this cold, see."

"Mr Whitt is a keen hymn singer," the Canon told her, his eyes twinkling at her.

"That's roight! Used to be in the choir when I be a lad."

"And talking of singing, Throssle Willy's just going to sing some of his ballads, on the stage we've set up near the barn. Let's go and see if he's started yet," the Canon explained, as they walked to the barn. "He had a beautiful bell-like soprano voice as a boy, we were very proud of him. He used to sing solos, in choir festivals in Bournemouth and Salisbury."

"The Canon paid for his singing lessons, an' all," Mr Whitt chimed in, as he hobbled along beside them.

The Canon ignored the interruption. "Now he has developed a rich baritone, and sings all around the Southwest, and on the radio too. He was known as 'Throstle Willy' as a child, because of his voice. It still sticks today. His voice gives us all great joy."

"Aye, no village 'ave got a throstle like ourrn," Mr Whitt grunted.

They could hear Throstle Willy before they could see him. For Kate, his full baritone filled the space. It reached a level where only her senses could follow, and then died away into a whisper of echoes. As his song ended his audience clapped and shouted deliriously, "come on, give us some morrre, Willy!" He was obviously the pride of the village. Kate watched him, lifting them away from threats and suspicions. The life they knew, was taking its usual shape again.

Throstle Willy broke into 'Because you come to me with nought save Lo-ove', and his audience cheered and yelled. This was obviously one of their favourites, thought Kate. Willy used all his singing technique, to give it everything he could. Kate turned to the Canon, whose face shone with pride. He then looked around them all, and could see that they no longer look stretched. "Bless you Willy for this," she heard him whisper.

*   *   *   *   *

"So, this is a new occupation for you, Squire."

John Gresham swung round and faced Wing Commander Cowper, the new owner of the village pub. "Not at all. I do the Aunt Sally here, every year. But of course, you're new to this village, and probably wouldn't know." David's eyebrows climbed half an inch, as he heard John Gresham's stern tone. This was a new John Gresham.

"It's good for my business, what," the Wing Commander's waxed moustache wax pulled up and down as he laughed. The brightness of his tie was striking.

"As you're here, you can help make it good for *our* business, couldn't he David! You could have 10 balls for five shillings. It is in aid of the heating for the church."

"What prize do I get, if I'm knock the hat off?"

"Any one of these things on the side table. It's not as easy as it looks. Behind that sacking, David is moving the hat all the time, backwards or forwards, whichever way he thinks, and at any pace he chooses. He varies all the time. Here's your five bobs' worth of balls."

After 10 misses, Wing Commander Cowper said, "well, I'd better go and show myself to the padre, just so as he knows that I've shown up. By the way, have you been taking any more morning walks lately, Squire?"

"I often walk over the Downs, at all sorts of times. I've done so all my life. So, I'm not quite sure what you mean." John Gresham did not trouble to hide his irritation.

"Don't you? The particular walk I was referring to, is when your red setter dog ran at my mare, in the lane that runs from Beech Farm to the gate on your estate wall. D'you remember?"

"Can't say I do."

"I'm not likely to forget it. It's made my mare bolt. Damn nearly threw me, had a hell of a job to get her quiet again. I'm surprised you don't remember."

"It must have been Rufus. He is a very impetuous dog, but he's getting better."

"It's about time, because that was nearly 6 months ago. I remember it was on the very next day, that your late wife was reported missing," Cowper said ominously.

John Gresham and David were stunned into silence.

The Wing Commander was obviously enjoying himself. He said: "I've often wondered what you were doing, going for walks at that time of the morning, and what it was that you'd lost. You looked as if you were looking for somebody, or something. It must have been between 10 and 11 in the morning, that's when I go for my rides, before opening time at the pub. Must keep fit you know. Nothing like a good old canter over the Downs, before starting in on the jug-and-bottle. But that's usually the time of the morning, that you're working indoors at your farm estate office, isn't it?"

"You seem to have made it your business to know my movements," said John Gresham.

"Not really. I know because your farm manager Harris is a buddy of mine. He's new here now, isn't he? He used to drink at my old pub in Bournemouth."

"I can't really remember what my routine was on that day, it's so long ago. I was probably trying to run a bit of steam off Rufus, he needed a lot of exercising in those days, that one.

To David's astonishment, John sounded as if he was defending himself.

"You looked to me as if you just come through the hedge from Beech farm Copse. You certainly looked surprised to see me, but then it's a lonely place isn't it. Then you're blasted dog ran at my mare. It all came back to me, as Sergeant Turner questioned me."

"Questioned you?"

"Oh yes. He plays around with questions and answers nearly every day. Having a great game with the village yokels. He calls it 'searching for information'. Didn't you know?"

"I'd no idea. Well I'm glad no harm came out of it, to you or your mare," John Gresham said with obvious effort.

"No, no harm came of it to *us*. Ah, there is the padre," and the Wing Commander left, with a flamboyant wave of his arm.

"What was all that about?" David asked.

"I... Only... wish... I knew."

David looked up suddenly at his tone. You saw the ice on John's lean handsome face, as he watched the retreating figure of the Wing Commander. His pupils were so dilated, it turned his eyes to black pools. Could they be pools of fear? Even his skin had turned grey, under his tan. Yes. The little lane behind their copse, he and Kate had discovered the other evening. The path that went through the copse, to the hole in the hedge. The other end of the lane, ran straight into the Gresham estate. That derelict cart-shed was the only building in sight.

John Gresham broke the silence. "He's an extraordinary chap. Never liked the fellow. One of those phoney Big-Heads. Too much of a city slicker for Larmer. He'll never be accepted here, he is too scornful of our country folk and their ways. God knows why he came. He should have stuck to his Bournemouth roadhouse."

They both turned to gather up the balls, and saw Frank Turner, the detective, standing close by. His burly figure in a light weight grey suit, looked less like a police officer for once. He appeared lost in his own thoughts, as he gazed at the tops of a clump of lime trees in the field opposite. He was watching a cloud of cawing rooks, rising and falling over them.

How long had he been there un-noticed, David wondered, and how much had he heard? He got the idea that Turner hadn't missed a thing, every detail had been registered by a brain very much awake, behind those friendly eyes. David heard John's sharp suck of breath, when he too suddenly saw Turner.

"Now, Sergeant Turner, are you going to throw caution to the winds, and have five shillings worth of shies at our Aunt Sally?" Anybody knowing John Gresham, would have been surprised to hear all this heartiness from him. Turner swung round, as if he had suddenly noticed them.

"Ah, nice to see you both. What a perfect afternoon. I was watching your rooks, they speak of autumn. I used to shoot them as a boy — verminous birds." No one ever looked less like a crime squad detective, at this moment. His friendly voice continued: "Yes, I'll have five shillings worth. Mind you, I'm no good at this sort of thing."

David said, "it's questions you're more used to firing, not shies." He made the joke to relieve tension.

When Turner had finished throwing his balls, he asked, "business pretty brisk?"

John Gresham seemed to swallow, and then said in a quiet voice, "oh yes, we are doing well. And what brings you here?"

"I just like to wander around, get the feel of the people and the place. It often leads you to the truth about them. For example, I get the feel here, of how devoted you all are to your Canon, and how he would never let any one of you down. I'll be seeing you, Mr Gresham, in Salisbury next Wednesday, won't I?"

"You will."

"Just a routine formality. Well, I'll wander along to hear Throstle Willy sing some of his songs. Goodbye for now."

David noticed this was another figure, whose retreat John Gresham watched with concern.

"How long do you think he'd been there, David?" he said casually, but his eyes looked strained.

"Hard to say. It's a bit tough though, how they come snooping round, even at a church fete. I'm getting pretty sick of them," said David.

"Like the rest of our village. Still, I suppose we've got to expect it, unto they clear this thing up."

"Why need anyone have done it? Why couldn't she just have fallen in, forgetting the well was there? Perhaps it was hidden by leaves."

"Because of that sheet of corrugated iron. Someone had put it there, after she had fallen through the well doors. That's why." There was bitterness in John Gresham's voice.

"Suppose someone had put corrugated iron there quite innocently, after the accident? Saw the rotted hole in the doors, and put it there as a safety measure, not knowing anything was in the well? Someone say, like the estate agent, before he sold it to us?"

"But Marion Ferguson told you she had put it there herself, before she left two years ago," John said quietly.

"Anyhow, it looks as if the police thought of that too, judging by the way everyone been questioned — every single person who ever had any connection with this place," David said.

"Ah!" The set of John Gresham's face cleared, as he saw one of his cow men approach. "Joe, come and have 5 shillings' worth on me. There is a 2 ounce package of tobacco still to be won. You won a gallon of beer last year, remember? Steady now, 10 shots." It was as if the threat of a moment ago, had never existed.

But all the time while David was behind the sacking, moving the hat perched on a stick, backwards and forwards for Joe's benefit, his thoughts were whirling. Yes, there was a nameless thing closing in on this village, and they must not let themselves get involved in any way, especially Kate, who was finding it tricky enough as it was. All this business had happened before he and Kate knew Larmer Magna existed. Whatever it was, none of it must be allowed to brush off onto them. They must stay outside it, until it was cleared up — difficult to do, because the Pendleton's, and everyone here, seemed so ready to accept them, in spite of their reputation to the contrary. But Kate was too vulnerable, he'd got to keep her right out of it, if they were ever to settle happily in Beech Farm. Such a decent chap, John Gresham...

*   *   *   *   *

It was a relief to be with Kate again, while they helped to clear up the mess, when the fete was over. He sensed her need to be near him now. They did all the jobs together.

They were helping Mrs Marsh stack crates of empty mineral bottles, when she suddenly stopped, and sat on one of them. She looked pale with heat.

"Leave it," Kate said. "You look so tired. David and I can easily finish it off."

"It's not that. I just wouldn't care if I never saw another crate again. There are stacks of them in our yard, outside our kitchen door, you can hardly move for 'em. These days, I seem to spend more time clearing them out of my kitchen, than I do in the shop. But give Harry his due, he does pile them up in his van, and take them back to the Red Lion, every time he's got a spare moment."

"You must sell a lot of minerals in your shop," Kate said.

"These aren't minerals, they're *beer*. The men won't drink in The Snug at the King John any more, they come and drink in our kitchen instead. They all pay into a kitty, then Harry takes the van to the Red Lion up at Newcombe and buys beer with it. I must say, they all leave and go home at the usual closing time, just as if it was a pub. Trouble is, we're landed with all those stacks of crates, it's nearly driving me mad."

"But why do they do this?"

"Oh, you know what men are. They say they can't talk freely in the pub anymore, because of Mr Moustachio listening in on one side of the bar, and that Sergeant Turner on the other side. So instead of drinking there in silence, they come and drink in our place, where there's no-one listening to what's being said. They've even brought the Dominos into our kitchen now."

At that moment, Harry joined them. As soon as his saw his wife, he roared with laughter. He slapped his knee with the joke, and called out to Bob Coe: "Hey, by golly Bob, come and look at this! The Missis, she's even sitting on them, now!"

Bob Cope came up grinning at Mrs Marsh.

"You should've seen old Bob a few days back in The Snug," Harry confided to David. "There we were, drinking our pints, and in slopes old Bob to join us. He suddenly sees that Sgt Turner at the bar, his eyes swivel right round, and he's out of that bar before you could say 'Bob Robinson'. Weren't you, my old pal?" A couple of other men had joined in the laugh at Bob by now.

"You know what it is, Harry," one of them said, "he's frightened Sergeant Turner saw him snaring rabbits the other night." They were all laughing again at Bob, whose only reaction to their ragging, was to stand silently by, wearing his huge grin.

"How do you find Mr Moustachio at the pub?" Harry asked David.

"We hardly know him — only seen him a couple of times."

"He's a real foreigner, you know. When he sees you passing, he calls out "Hello, how are you." Ga! He don't care how you are, so what's the silly fool asks you for?" It was Kate and David's turn to laugh.

As Sergeant Turner strolled into view, Harry said jauntily, "I'd best be going indoors to count that pile of money. I reckon we've taken more here this afternoon, than our shop takes in six months." He explained proudly to Kate and David, "I be the Treasurer, see."

By the time Sergeant Turner reached them, the whole group had scattered, only Kate and David were left.

"Can I help you at all?" Turner asked in his pleasant friendly voice.

"You certainly can," said David. "Could you help me carry all of these crates of empties, and load of them up in the Land Rover? The driver's waiting to take them back to the store at Ludlow Hollow, 4 miles away."

The little knot of people standing by the Land Rover, joking with the driver, melted away as David and Turner staggered up with the crates. They stacked them until the Land Rover was full.

As they walked back to join Kate, Turner said, "it's a dreary job being a detective in a village like this. Where ever I go, people move away..." and yet he grinned at David.

His grin hung in the air, like a cloud on a sunny day. David looked at him, but said nothing.

15. The evening after the village fete

When the mess of the fete was all cleared up, the Pendleton's invited all the helpers into the Rectory for a drink. Sums of money were being counted in the long white panelled drawing-room by Harry, sitting by the wall opposite the three deep windows, which opened onto the garden, and grass tennis court. Every time Harry counted another £10 that topped last year's takings, he gave a great shout of glee. Gradually, everyone in the room gathered round him, in the triumph as he counted.

The Canon had given David the job of handing round drinks, and keeping them topped up. As he did so, he could feel the warmth and closeness between these people, as they grouped together. At least here they were free of the police presence, and 'gibbet sickness.' Barriers were no longer needed, issues were no longer confused, safety surged around them.

He could see Kate and Jane Lloyd laughing and talking over their gins. He went to them and topped up their drinks. "And don't toss those down your beautiful throats, in a way that shows people that you have a talent for drinking," he laughed, and passed on. It was good to see Kate collecting a friend of her own age.

He was topping up another drink in the middle of the room, when suddenly he stopped. He could hear John Gresham's quiet but bitter voice immediately behind him, saying to the Canon: "Yes, it is true. The inquest is to be re-opened. But this time, the Coroner will have a jury, and doubtless teams from The Crime Squad, not to mention a covey from the Press. It wouldn't surprise me if your Richard turns up from Scotland Yard, too. According to Turner, Williams and he were both going to interview Ashley Wentworth, in Town."

"The net is spreading pretty wide, isn't it. I'll be there with you at the inquest, John. This is no time for a man to be alone." David heard the Canon's quiet assurance.

David moved quickly back to Kate, and took her arm. "Darling, it's time to take you home, to get my dinner. The rumblings of my inner man are becoming peremptory, and loud."

*   *   *   *   *

"Let's go for a stroll, and make the most of this perfect evening," David suggested to Kate, after they have finished their meal. "We can clear up from this meal when we get back, and it's dark."

He held her hand as they stood in the drive outside the front door. They could feel the brush of the evening, as the moths flew by. At the end of the lawn, a larch tree made a wispy green-black silhouette against the sky. Beech trees were rustling, and sleepy birds settling, with dreamy cheeps. Altogether they seemed to breathe peace at this moment, which nothing could disturb — not even the hoots from the owls, or the barking of a fox.

They wandered up the garden towards the beech copse in silence, and felt the stillness. Their lives were complete. They stopped and watched a belated bee still buzzing among the ragwort.

"You can almost see his breath blowing on the flowers," Kate said in a whisper.

David kissed the top of her head. "That's one of the zany things I love about you," he laughed.

They strolled through the copse to the summer house. They pushed open the door, and looked inside. It looked as neglected, and as empty, as a church on a Monday afternoon.

"Well obviously, no one's been here since we last came, it looks no different," David said as he shut the door.

"Why? Did you expect someone to have come?"

"One never knows. Let's just walk along the path to the lane."

They pushed through the hole in the hedge, and stood in the lane for a while, looking up and down it. Then they started to walk up it, in the direction of the Gresham estate. The lane became a flint and chalk track crossing the downland slope, and overhead was the weep and wail of plovers, and the cry of the curlews. There was a wide view of rolling hills in the fading light. David felt as if he needed some width tonight.

"Listen Kate, you and I have got to make our own stand in this 'Well' thing. I know it happened on our land, but still it has nothing to do with us. Our stand must be one of non-involvement with anybody, otherwise we are going to get hung up on it, and perhaps risk being mighty miserable, as a result."

"How do you mean, make a stand?"

"Stay right outside everybody who tries to discuss it with you, or involve your sympathy. Don't give opinions, remain politely aloof. Above all, don't get too friendly with any of them, even the Pendletons."

"But that means isolationism," said Kate.

"It does, until they've solved the crime. It'll be very grim for us, if it is finally pinned on someone we'd learnt to like. At the moment, don't let's like anybody. Let's stay outside them all, and get on with doing our house."

"Something's happened, David. What is it?"

"Nothing has. It's just a precautionary measure," he avoided her eyes.

"But I'm spending the day with Jane Lloyd on Tuesday. Does that mean I can't go?"

She looked so crestfallen. He slipped his arm round her. "Fine, you go and enjoy it. But keep off discussions about this, stick to the usual channels of chat."

"Like swapping side-effects of the pill?" she giggled.

"You see..." he stopped and stood gazing thoughtfully at the forest trees in the Manor Park.

"Yes, David, something *has* happened. It's not fair not to tell me."

"It's just that it's coming too near to us. That Cowper character who owns the pub, spoke of Sergeant Turner snooping around the village. He's gradually building up a tremendous case against someone, at present of unknown identity. Cowper could even be one of Turner's pawns, planted to prod admissions out of unsuspecting people, but how do we know? They'll play any trick to get at the truth, they almost have to. The whole village is heavy with it, especially with Turner wandering among them so obviously. It seems they're all watching him, out of the corner of their eyes, while they live with fear, and in silence."

"It came through to me too, this afternoon," said Kate. "I was thankful for Throssle Willy's songs, along with the rest of them. When they weren't jabbering on, they all looked as if they were waiting for something to strike."

"Doom, as it were?"

"Right, you could call it that."

"These village people are so closely knit together, even though they're full of whispers, not one sound of it will reach police ears. No one can believe its extent, until they came to live among it. I imagine the police methods, have to be to stick around, poking into everything, until they get these people watching, looking over their shoulders, until a breaking point is reached. And they probably use outsiders, to lead them to the weak links."

"Cowper, you mean?"

"Yes. We have to be on our guard, in case they try to use us. I think sometimes, the detection of crime is crueller than the crime itself. But we must never let ourselves be used, or our loyalties pulled. We've *got* to remain impartial, and not dragged in. It'd be too easy to become part of the murmuring community."

"This crime crouches over the village, just as much as the Downs do," Kate said miserably.

"It's got nothing to do with us. Let's go home, Darling".

"I wish 'going home', meant anywhere but Beech Farm, now," Kate said unhappily. David said nothing.

As they reached the summerhouse, David saw he must have left the door slightly open, yet he could have sworn that he had shut it. It fitted very tightly, so this time he gave it a good bang. Promptly, startled birds squawked, and fluttered from the trees. But also, they could hear the snapping of twigs, as human feet stepped hurriedly over them. Instinctively, they both ran to the part of the copse where the sound came from, just in time to see a figure lurching and shambling unsteadily, as it slipped hastily through the trees. When they caught up with the figure, they found it was Jimmy. Spittle was drooling out of his mouth, his vacant eyes rolling with terror. He leant against one of the trees, choking to get back his breath, then made a terrible noise in his throat, like a dog growling.

"What the hell are you doing on my land?" David shouted at him. "Clear off this minute. D'you hear?!"

Jimmy shuffled towards the lane. They watched him make straight for the opening in the hedge — yes, he knew exactly where it was. "And don't come back here again, or you'll be in dead trouble!" David shouted after him.

They both went back to the summerhouse in silence. They looked inside it again, but in the deepening dusk, could see nothing that had been disturbed.

"David, did you ever tell the detective about this hut, and the path, and the hole in the hedge to the lane?"

"No."

"Why not? You said you were going to."

"I don't know why not. Anyway, I didn't."

"Are you going to?" asked Kate.

"I don't know, I suppose I'll have to," he said wretchedly. "Kate, it means they'll come sprawling all over our garden, right up to here. They'll be nothing of it left for us anymore."

"Is that the only reason?"

"No... not exactly."

"So, what's all this guff about keeping ourselves apart, and impartial? David, Darling, you're becoming as much a part of the close ranks of this community as I am. You're hung up on them too, but you're not admitting it. The difference is, I don't want to be hung up on them, but I can't help myself. That's one reason why I hate the place. For me, it's all loused up."

She saw his face, and tucked her hand into his, as they walked home in the light of rising moon. They stood in the drive for a long moment, before going indoors.

<u>16. The plot thickens as the police investigate</u>

"Right then. I'll leave investigating Marion Ferguson until the last. I'll follow up the other frayed bits of thread first, and see what turns up from them," Williams thought, as his train drew out of Waterloo Station, towards Salisbury.

He settled back into his corner seat, and unfolded his newspaper, as the train gathered speed. He turned the pages — all the usual bellyaching, from one page to the next. The pound was tottering yet again, the Cabinet appeared to be a bunch of halfwits, soccer was turning into an international punch-up, increase in abortion in the under sixteens, the housing scandal... it never stopped. Any foreigner reading our daily papers would think that Britain was falling apart, he though. They never mentioned the peerless humane standards of British Justice in our Law Courts, unmatched by the whole world.

He folded the paper, and looked out of the window. Thick cords of rain were slashing across, slamming at the window by his elbow, and then wriggling across the glass. Yes, he'd leave Marion Ferguson until the last. It wasn't that Pendleton had tried to deflect him from his duty. The chap had even said, "you must do exactly as you think fit, Inspector." In any case, the other frayed ends had to be investigated as well, it was just a matter of changing the order around. But all the same, he had backed out of handling the case, when he saw where it could lead him. Quite right too.

A man's personal life must never overlap a case he was working on. If it did, he could no longer act objectively, and that was essential for real justice. He would have done the same himself. But he had no personal life, not since Mary had been killed in a motor smash two years after their marriage. He was over it now; it had been about seven years, and he'd pitched everything he'd got into his work, and forging ahead.

But all the same, there was something about this case that he just couldn't pin down. A feeling, a sniff of something. 'Intuition George', they'd nicknamed him in the crime squad. Right now, all his tentacles were out, but he couldn't see in what direction to go. He just felt it. Richard Pendleton and Marion Ferguson? What had the Canon learned from Jimmy the lad with learning difficulties? John Gresham, and that snide reference about him possibly remarrying, coming from Ashley Wentworth. But this could be just bitchiness?

Was Marion Ferguson involved with Richard Pendleton? If so, why had they not married, surely anyone might well have fallen for him? And anyhow, what had that got to do with this case? Look how Mary had fallen for an ordinary chap like himself. Enough fellows were after her, so forget it.

But for no logical reason, the rhythm of the train kept hammering through his head. Richard Pendleton... Marion Ferguson... John Gresham...

*	*	*	*	*

Williams went straight from the train to Salisbury Police Headquarters. "Sergeant Turner about?" he asked as immediately as he got in.

"No Sir, he's out at Larmer," the duty officer on the desk replied.

"Please get him on the phone, and ask him to get through to me, as soon as he can."

"Yes Sir. There's a note on your desk regarding the inquest on Amanda Gresham. It's to be re-opened on Wednesday at midday."

All the time he was drinking coffee in his office, Williams' fingers were tapping on his blotter. He was thinking hard. How could the Canon's support for the village be swung to the side of the police? How could he be persuaded to say what Jimmy had revealed? Surely the principle of Law and Justice, was as important as the principle of the Sanctity of the Confessional? No, not to a parson, and such a man. Perhaps he could work on John Gresham, to persuade the Canon... after all, they were great friends, and it was his wife's murder that they were trying to solve. The solution lay dead centre in the heart of Larmer, he was convinced of that.

Why had Marion Ferguson run away? Was it out of loneliness? After all, she had gone a whole year and a half before Amanda Gresham was murdered.

His buzzer rang. "Yes, Williams here. Frank?" he listened intently. "Sounds interesting. Right, I'll wait here for you. See you in half an hour."

A bit of a lead had come to light at last — and at the rectory garden fete of all places! Good man, Frank.

*   *   *   *   *

"Good to see you, Sir. How was London?" Frank asked as he came in.

"No direct leads. Only offshoots from the case as far as I can see, and the discovery that Amanda Gresham was wanton and woolly, and rather wild."

"What about Ashley Wentworth?"

"I went with DS Pendleton to interview him, as you know. Nothing there. Pendleton likes him as much as a tiger likes a snake. Frank," he leaned forwards intently. "I'm convinced the solution lies here in Larmer, and nowhere

191

else. Now let's have your bit of a lead, that's come to light."

"D'you remember when we interviewed John Gresham at the Manor, right at the start of this enquiry, you asked him quite definitely what his movements had been on the morning of his wife's disappearance. Here it is," he pulled out his notebook. "You said, 'So you went straight from the Manor to your estate office, and never left until you returned to the Manor at teatime,' and Gresham replied, 'yes that's right.'"

"I remember."

"I noted how you rather pressed that point at the time. His statement was untrue, Sir. I heard him admit it at the Rectory fete last Saturday. Not only that. He was seen coming out of Beech Farm copse, onto the lane that runs around the back, to his own estate wall." Turner went on to report the conversation he had overheard, between Wing Commander Cowper and John Gresham.

"Have you questioned John Gresham about it yet?"

"No Sir. I thought it better to leave it to you, when you got back. I did go to the farm office, and questioned his farm manager about his employer's movements that morning, in a casual sort of way, so as not to rouse more of those damned village loyalties. It's quite true. Gresham did leave the farm office soon after 10 o'clock, and did not return until about midday. The bloke remembered it quite easily — remembering fuming around, waiting for him to come back, to discuss some papers. He'd got the vet in at the time, to help with a difficult calving, and he was on his toes to join him in the cowshed, but he couldn't leave till his boss came back. His name is Harris. He is not a local man, comes from 30 miles away in Hampshire. That's far enough to cast him as 'a foreigner' with this village. They don't dislike him, but he holds himself aloof from them, and they respect him as a good farmer. But on the other hand, they don't trust his acquaintance with the Wing Commander at the pub."

"I see you've got Harris sorted out. Good work," Williams interrupted with a laugh. He stopped laughing and scratched his head. He said slowly, "we don't know *why* John Gresham misled us in his statement about his movements that morning, but it's a fact that he *did* so. It may be nothing to do with the crime, just a personal matter that he doesn't want us poking into."

"Like having diarrhoea, Sir." They both laughed.

"It must have been a fierce dose of squitters to take an hour and a half! Frank, it doesn't look good when a man misleads the police."

"This brings me to the next thing, Sir. I heard someone say in the Snug that Jimmy, the lad with learning difficulties, had been hanging round the kitchen door at the Manor, from early morning that day. He wanted to see Amanda Gresham. He wouldn't leave, even when they tried to shoo him off pretty forcibly."

"Did he see her in the end?"

"He did, before she went out."

"Then let's go out to Larmer now, and go ourselves to the kitchen door, and question some of the staff. They might even drop a few crumbs. We won't go and see John Gresham until after the inquest. You've done well, Frank — a darned sight better than I did in London." Or, it occurred to him, had he done rather better than he thought?

*   *   *   *   *

"Mr Taylor, the two detective gentlemen are here," Mrs Clark the housekeeper called out over her shoulder. She held the door open. "You'd better come in, Sir," she said to them both. She showed them into a plain but comfortably furnished kitchen. A bowl of flowers which looked as if it had been flung together, stood on the centre of the kitchen table. A radio was blaring away the current top twenty.

Taylor the manservant appeared, and Mrs Clark went out of the room. He was formal and dignified. He first switched off the radio, and then greeted his visitors. "Can I help you in any way, gentlemen?"

"I think you can. We came to ask you about the morning Jimmy came to this kitchen door, wanting to see Mrs Gresham. In fact, he wanted to see her so badly, that he just wouldn't leave. Is that so?" Williams asked.

"It is. It was on the morning of the day of her disappearance. Mrs Gresham was still in bed, she hadn't finished her breakfast. It was one of the times when she... wasn't very well."

"Would you have any idea why he was so anxious to see her?"

"I'm afraid I haven't. It's impossible to understand what he was trying to say."

"But Mrs Gresham could understand him?" asked Williams.

"Yes, up to a point. It's curious that she could. Perhaps it's because he hung around her so much, she got to recognise what his sounds meant. The Canon can understand him a bit, too. None of the rest of us can make out a word of it."

"What did you do with him, on that occasion?"

"When he refused to go, and started making those awful screeching noises at us, Mrs Clark the housekeeper went up to Mrs Gresham to tell her what was happening. It was the only thing to do. Would you like Mrs Clark to come in and tell you about it, herself?"

"Yes, thank you, we would," said Williams.

Taylor got up with quiet dignity, opened the kitchen door and called to Mrs Clark, who had obviously been listening outside the door. She looked at Taylor as she came in, as she would look at a fly that had dropped into her soup. She then turned her belligerent eyes on the two detectives. She had a thin, bitter mouth, and was obviously not going to stand for any nonsense from anybody, police or whatever. Taylor clearly and briefly put the problem before her, as if she hadn't already heard every word of it.

She said, "well, I went straight up and told Mrs Gresham, bless her. She had brought me down here to this wretched place, when she married Mr Gresham. I used to serve in the Wentworth house in London. Sir Roger Wentworth was her father, you know." Her tone implied that all the Gresham's together didn't have a title amongst them. She folded her hands and gave a disdainful sniff.

"Yes," Mrs Clark gave another sniff. "Mrs Gresham insisted on having me here with her. She couldn't stand that awful Nanny Bridget — she just had to get rid of her. I came and took over the housekeeping, in her place."

Taylor quietly explained, "Nanny Bridget had been Mr John's nanny, when he was a baby. When he grew out of the nursery, she became housekeeper here. Both of Mr John's parents were sadly killed in a plane accident in Italy, and she took over the whole domestic running of the Manor. She did it extremely well, and very happily for all of us. Mr John was in his last year at Cambridge, when the tragedy of his parents' death happened. I don't know what he, or any of us as far as that goes, would have done without Nanny Bridget. She was always known as that, long after she stopped being Mr John's nanny. She is very Irish, Sir."

"Was she here at the time Jimmy was so anxious to see Mrs Gresham?"

"That she was not! She soon had to go when Mrs Gresham arrived in Larmer Manor, I can tell you," said Mrs Clark. "She wouldn't have had that woman about the place, with her bossy ways, and her Irish moods. That's when I arrived instead," Mrs Clark's eyes glittered at the memory, and her folded hands tightened, as they rested on her stomach.

"Where is Nanny Bridget now?" Williams asked Taylor.

"She's at the Rectory. Mr John was very upset when Nanny Bridget told him she wouldn't stay on, not even to please him — not with Mrs Gresham. Mr John couldn't see her leave Larmer altogether, not after all these years, and after what we've all been through together — she was part of his life. So Canon and Mrs Pendleton offered her a position as housekeeper at the Rectory, must be seven years ago now. She's been very happy there, and a pleasure for them. It means Mr John can go and see her any time, which he does quite often. It has worked out very well."

"And she never comes here to the Manor?" asked Williams.

"Never set foot in it since. She wouldn't come while Mrs Gresham, and of course Mrs Clark, were here." This last was said by Taylor, with great dignity. He didn't often get a chance like this.

"Well now, let's get back to Jimmy," Williams said. "Did Mrs Gresham see him that morning?"

"Yes, she did," Mrs Clark was quite definite. "She'd just finished her breakfast when I went up to her. She told me to take her tray away, and to tell Jimmy to wait. He hung round the stables, until she was ready. I saw her go out to him. Then she seemed to get very excited while she talked to him. She came running into the house and fetched her riding whip. I thought she must be going to take her two dogs out with her, as she always took her riding whip with her then — but she didn't. She dashed out of the house again, next thing I saw her running down the drive, alone."

"In the direction of the village?"

"Yes, and Jimmy shambling after her, way behind. He couldn't keep up with the pace she was going. It must have been something very important, for her to go blinding off like that," Mrs Clark added.

"Perhaps it was all part of her recent nervous attack," Williams said, watching her face intently for her reaction.

"Oh no, I've seen plenty of those, the poor lamb. This was very different — quite different. Even Jimmy seemed excited."

"You didn't miss much, did you! You must have been watching every move she made," Turner observed.

"I always did. And that day, she was not very well. She needed looking after, my pretty one. I was the only person who cared — the *only* person," she said significantly.

"What happened after that?"

"She blinded down the drive as if... it was life and death. I just waited for her to come back... Excuse me, Sir..." and Mrs Clark went from the room in tears.

"Poor woman," Taylor said. "In spite of everything, I can't help feeling sorry for her. She was devoted to Mrs Gresham, and now she won't have anything moved in her bedroom or sitting room. Everything's there, just as if she was coming back at any moment. She cleans the room herself, and I believe she turns down the bed every night, and draws the curtains."

"How about Mr Gresham — does she get on with him?"

"He never sees her, really. He made it pretty clear that he didn't want to more than necessary, after she replaced Nanny Bridget."

"Did Mr Gresham go out too that morning?" Williams asked casually.

"Oh yes. He went down to the farm office, straight after breakfast. He always does when he's not in London."

"Did he return here during the morning, at all?"

"I think he did. Yes, now I come to think of it, he did. He whistled for Rufus the dog, for a bit of a run."

Williams exchanged a glance with Turner. "And he too went down the drive with Rufus?"

"Oh no, Sir. He went the other way."

"How can you remember this? It was four months ago!"

"Because I remember thinking 'isn't this typical. Mrs Gresham goes out walking in one direction, and half an hour later Mr John goes walking in the opposite direction'. You must pardon me saying this, but they were opposites in everything".

"Marriages are often like that. But you're sure it was on that morning he went out?"

"Yes Sir. Harris kept ringing up from the farm office, to see if he was back yet."

Williams and Turner again exchanged glances. "What time did he go out?"

"I can't say exactly. It must be some time between 10 and 11 a.m."

"Where did he go?"

"Oh, just out to give Rufus a run, anywhere."

"Did you see Jimmy again that day?" asked Williams.

"We certainly did! He came back here later in the morning, crying and crying. A horrible sort of guttural, choking sound. He made a real nuisance of himself with it. We couldn't think what had possessed him — he really did seem possessed. In the end, we couldn't stand it and we got the gardener to take him home."

"If only we could know what Jimmy was telling Mrs Gresham! That's the whole, the vital clue. And there's no one left who can understand him."

"Oh, there is Sir. There's the Canon," said Taylor.

"Yes, the Canon," Williams said bitterly. "Thank you again for your help Mr Taylor. We'll be coming to see Mr John Gresham again soon."

*　　*　　*　　*　　*

As they drove away, Williams said, "so there we are. We now have three independent pieces of evidence, corroborating one thing — John Gresham *did* go out for a walk that morning. Mr John Gresham is our next call, but not until after the inquest, in case he makes any statement there first. He snapped his jaws together, in a way that would have done credit to a crocodile.

17. The police investigate further

"I didn't make an appointment with John Gresham, Frank," Williams said as they drove out to Larmer. "I thought it better to take a chance on it, and his being totally unprepared. We might be unlucky and find him out, or gone away, but some how I don't think so. Not after seeing his face in the Coroner's Court when they returned a verdict of 'Murder by Persons Unknown'. It must take a bit of swallowing. I'd think it more likely he'd go straight home from the Court."

"To safety and security?"

"That's about it, for that kind of chap. One couldn't help feeling sorry for him."

"Yup! It's a cruel game tracing crime to conviction. But you only get stuck with that feeling, if you let yourself get involved with the personalities concerned," said Turner.

Williams grinned at Frank's purposeful stolid face as he drove, his eyes never wavering from the road ahead.

"Okay Frank! I asked for that".

They both laughed. They were getting to understand one another uncommonly well, forming an efficient team. If he was moved on, he'd certainly take Frank along with him, if he'd come.

*   *   *   *   *

"Will you come in, Sir. I'll see if Mr Gresham can see you,, said Taylor the manservant, as if he had never seen them so recently.

He soon returned. "Mr Gresham will see you, please come this way, Sir."

He led them through a long gallery, with full-length oil paintings of the Gresham ancestors. One was a handsome man in a Charles II curly wig, whose face could have been a portrait of the present John Gresham. He even had the same long sensitive hands. How these blueblood characters keep on reproducing themselves. Pity there were no children to continue the line.

They were shown into the garden room, which was quite small, with modern furniture in bright colours. One wall was made entirely of sliding glass panels, which were pushed back, so that the room opened straight onto a flagstone terrace. A flight of stone steps led down from the terrace, to a large pond, or small artificial lake below. A fountain was splattering in its centre. Two ducks were gliding in and out of the spray.

Williams looked around him. This must be at the back of the house, so unseen from the main entrance, and from the sides. Beyond the lake, were ancient cedars and copper beeches standing beyond a lawn. Behind them were deep woods, stretching up to the Downs. It was a beautiful, undisturbed bit of England. John Gresham was stretched out on a garden chair. Good manners made him get up and greet the two men.

"We're sorry to disturb you, Mr Gresham," Williams said.

"Yes, I can't think of a worse time to come," John Grisham replied wearily. "I'd have thought that whatever you've come for, could wait until tomorrow, under the circumstances." Hostility made his tone decisive. There was a cold bleak look on his face.

"Crime can't wait, where crime is involved," Williams said crisply. That hard, taut line was back in his jaw. "The pity is, you yourself have made this visit necessary, I'm sorry to say."

"Oh?" said John Gresham, enquiringly.

"Yes, you've made a misleading statement to us, on our last visit to you. I'm afraid I have no alternative now, but to check on it."

Without a word, John Gresham motioned them both to two garden chairs, then lay back on his own. His face was dull and empty, as he scanned the dark woods beyond, and waited for the detectives to continue.

"You stated that on the morning of the day Mrs Gresham disappeared, you went down to your estate farm office immediately after breakfast, and has never left it again, until you came back here to the Manor, about teatime. You even had your lunch down there."

"I did — that's what I did. I had a great deal of estate business to get through," he said in a flat tired tone.

"I also asked you, with quite a lot of emphasis, whether you left the estate office at all, at any time during the morning. Your reply was that you did not," said Williams.

"That's right. Well?"

"This time I want you to think very carefully before answering. Did you, or did you not, leave the estate office at any time that morning, between the hour of your arrival, at lunchtime?"

There was a long silence while John Gresham with glazed eyes, watched the ducks ferrying across the lake. He crossed his legs and looked at Williams. "I don't believe I left it — it's difficult to remember".

"That's not what you said the first time. Then, you were quite definite, that you never left it at all during the morning."

"What are you trying to make me say, Inspector?"

"Just the truth, Mr Gresham."

"I see," he said slowly. "What makes you think my first statement was not the truth?"

"Because we've had statements from three different sources, corroborating each other, that you was seen walking out of doors between the hours of 10 and 11:30 that morning. And in the direction of Beech Farm." His eyes were as cold as ice.

"What gives you the right not only to go snooping round my farm estate office, questioning my farm manager behind my back, but to intrude even into my own kitchen, questioning my people? I'd have thought my permission should have been asked first."

"It's been done for the right of finding the criminal who murdered your wife, Mr Gresham. But you still haven't answered my question. Did you, or did you not, go out that morning?"

"I may have done. I don't really remember. Yes, I believe I did, come to think of it. I took my setter Rufus for a walk." He threw a quick, wary glance at Turner.

"It's strange that you didn't 'come to think of it', when I first stressed the point to you, just over a week ago."

"You've never experienced it, Inspector, but it's very difficult to keep every movement you've ever made a few months ago, clear in your mind, when you've just heard your wife's body has been found down a well."

Williams ignored his sarcasm. "So now we've got a different statement from you. You admit you did go out between the hours of 10 and 11:30 that morning?"

"I suppose so," he said wearily.

"You must be definite, Mr Gresham. You've already tried to mislead the police, by one false statement. That does not help your position in the case. Neither does it help you to be a hostile witness, in the attempt to solve your wife's murder."

"As you wish. Yes, I took Rufus for a walk at that time."

"In which direction did you go?"

For a moment, the glaze dropped away, and John Gresham looked at Williams, as he would at a tiger who had suddenly padded onto the terrace. "I went through the woods you see ahead of you, and then onto the Downs behind. Yes, it does curl round in the direction of the back of Beech Farm copse, and then onto the main Shaftesbury Road. I came back the same route," he said in a tight voice, part of the line of his mouth showed him to be a fighter, on his guard.

"It's a strange thing, more than that, a suspicious thing, the way you can now remember all the details so clearly, when a moment ago, you could hardly remember. What are you trying to hide Mr Gresham?"

"I don't have to put up with this infernal rudeness from you, Inspector. Please be good enough to stick strictly to your questioning, and then leave my house. It can't be too soon for me."

His blustering only showed Williams to what extent he was on the defensive.

"Your statements conflict so much in the space of a few moments, Mr Gresham, that it can only point to the fact that your hiding something. This is very dangerous for the whole exercise in pursuit of *truth*, which you seem reluctant to tell. So now we have established the fact that you *did* go out that morning to take your dog for a walk, in the direction of Beech Farm."

"Yes, but why do you make all this fuss over it?"

Williams looked at him searchingly. "I have to remind you, Mr Gresham," he said slowly and emphatically, "that your wife was last seen alive at 10 o'clock that morning, and she too went out, and was not seen again until her body was found down the well, at Beech Farm."

"So you think I pushed my wife down the well at Beech Farm, is that it? And that I did it between the hours of 10 and 11:30? You didn't know her, Inspector. No one could push Amanda around anywhere she didn't want to go. It was she who did the pushing." His face was twisted with bitterness. "As a matter of interest, and of course you're bound to know, where did she go for her walk?"

"Down the drive, then up the village street, also in the direction of Beech Farm."

"Incredible... and I didn't see her," he said wonderingly.

Williams looked at him quickly. Either this was genuine surprise, or the fellow was a superb actor. There was no telling from his face, which still had that frozen look.

"Any more questions Inspector, or have you about finished?" John Gresham was crossing and uncrossing his legs impatiently.

"Just one more. What was the purpose of your walk?"

"I've told you, to exercise my setter dog. He'd got a lot of steam to run off in those days, he was only eight months old then." That wary look was back again.

"Yet it seems very odd that you should decide to exercise him at that moment. Your farm manager, Harris, told us he had one of your pedigree cows calving, with a difficult breech, and he had to call in the vet to help. The vet was in the cowshed doing the job at that time, because Harris had to go back to the farm office to clear up estate business with you. You knew Harris was in a hurry to get back to the cowshed, yet you chose that very moment to stop work, and keep him waiting, while you took your dog for a walk for an hour and a half. Can you explain this?"

His tortured eyes stared at Williams. "I'm not prepared to, and I don't have too, Inspector."

"It'd be better for your own sake if you did. You're placing yourself in a tricky position, by hiding the reason for this walk at such a time. It must be something of great importance to you."

"I don't have to account to you, for every private thought of my life. You overreach yourself, Inspector."

"On that day, I'm afraid you do, if only to clear yourself as a suspect, of being implicated in your wife's murder. If this comes to Court, you would certainly have to account for every moment, before a judge."

"Whatever makes you think that was the time she was murdered?"

"We don't know for certain. But we do have the evidence of the inconsolable grief of Jimmy, the lad with learning difficulties, when he returned to the kitchen entrance without her. He was seen by your staff, and it was quite certainly before midday. Before that, they saw him follow her as she left for a walk in a hurry, at 10 o'clock, after which she was never seen again," Williams stared thoughtfully at the small lake. "She was found to have died from drowning."

John Gresham followed the direction of his gaze. "So, you think I left the farm office to lie in wait for my wife, drowned her in this small lake, and then pushed her body down Beach Farm well." He suddenly laughed. "The lake of all places! We had a bit of trouble over this lake. She insisted on having it made, when the village went on to mains water about four years ago. I resisted it, as it seemed to me out of place, but of course she got her way in the end. I was even thinking of filling it in again, just as you arrived." He gave a bitter laugh. "While you're working on this case, I'd have thought you could cook up something better than that."

"If you genuinely want to solve your wife's murder, perhaps you could stop laying these tales of suspicion behind yourself, and be more cooperative with the work we have to do."

"I've been all the help I can, Inspector. There's nothing further I can do for you. There's no point in prolonging this visit. I've had a tiring day," he said through tight lips. "So goodbye."

As Williams and Turner got up to go, Williams said over his shoulder, "one last thing, Mr Gresham. Did you see anybody on your walk that morning? If you did, it would be an alibi to clear your actions between the hours are 10 and midday."

"I have nothing further to say to you, Inspector."

*　　*　　*　　*　　*

As soon as the two detectives had gone, John Gresham closed the door, and telephoned the number of Christopher Mainwaring, the Chief Constable of the county.

"Chris, this is John Gresham here. It's most important I have a word with you. Yes, as soon as possible. You can? You can guess of course, what it's about. Yes, today. Fine. On your way home, I'll expect you about 6:30. I'm most grateful."

*   *   *   *   *

Later that day, the two men sat on the same terrace, with their drinks beside them. Chris was saying, "yes, I'm beginning to quite like the lake after all. It doesn't look too bad, John, in spite of all the bother you had with her over it."

John Gresham considered the square face of the Chief Constable beside him. He had put on a bit of weight. The serious face of Chris, whom as a boy he had known at school, was growing heavy, and jowled. He said, "I'll come straight to the point, Chris. I'd be grateful if you could use your authority and influence, to stop those two moronic detectives from pestering me."

"In what way are they doing so?"

"Well first, they go snooping round my estate farm office, questioning my farm manager about my movements..."

"Your movements when John?"

"On the morning of the day that Amanda disappeared."

"I see. Go on," said the Chief Constable.

"And next thing, they invade my kitchen, questioning my people behind my back, about my movements."

"Not altogether. Be fair, John. The main purpose of their visit to the kitchen, was to check up on Amanda's movements before she died, and how Jimmy came into it. The check on your own movements, it was just an additional thing that came out of it."

"How do you know this?"

"I've instructed them to report back to me, in everything they do. Because it's you, old chap, I feel very closely concerned with this case. I want it cleared up for you, and quickly. I can't have my men missing a thing, not that those two would, in any case. We are lucky to have Williams on the job, he has a brilliant record, and is on his way up to high places. He has that rare quality, a good imagination, that manages to be perceptive as well. It gives him a particular kind of flair, in his work. And Turner is as reliable as they come."

"That's all very fine. But surely man, they should ask my permission first, before snooping round my property, and questioning my people."

The Chief Constable's eyes opened wide. He sipped his whisky, and watched the ice clink against his glass, as his swirled it around. At last he said, "why should any man mind, if his movements and motives are completely honest, and above board. I don't think they needed your permission. Anybody has a right to call on anybody."

"And ask questions about their employer?"

"The questions about you, were only part of many other routine inquiries they have to make. John, can't you see? They're not accusing you, they're trying to clear you of suspicion of being involved in this crime. And God only knows, if you'd been involved, there was motive enough in your case."

"You mean the money, I suppose," John said with bitterness.

"No, I don't, you ass! I mean that what you've put up with for so many years, is more than the average man could take. Loneliness is a hell of thing."

"Surely, if I was going to kill her, I'd have done so years ago."

"Not necessarily."

"Chris! *I did not kill her*! You must believe that," John said quietly, and emphatically.

"I do, old chap. But the problem is, that you yourself have laid your own trail of suspicion. Look at it from their point of view. You state in the first place, that you never left the farm office all morning, and only left it at teatime. You even assured Williams that was the truth, when he first stressed the point. Then they found that this was a false statement, and that you *did* go out. You were seen in the vicinity of Beech Farm, at a vital point of time, when it is believed that Amanda was killed — and at Beech Farm. They can't dismiss this. Of course, they have to follow it up, especially when you won't help them yourself, by telling them just what you would doing, where you went, and why. You're even blocking their way, John, and this doesn't look good for you, especially on top of your false statement."

"Just whose side are you on, Chris?"

"Yours, of course, if you're innocent. But my officers are doing their duty, and I have to support them, in their proper execution of this. They have a job of work to do, they're doing it efficiently, and conscientiously. I've shown myself to be on your side, and I have instructed them to find all the evidence they can, to clear you of implication. It is you, old chap, who's standing in their way of being able to do it."

"By not answering all the questions?"

"Yes, and by conflicting statements. It makes it seem obvious to them, that you are hiding something, at the the key moment in this case. Can't you see how disturbing that is, John?"

"They even asked me for an alibi — did I go and see anybody, when I took my dog Rufus for a walk? And in the hearing of Taylor, as he showed them out. I think it's deplorable."

"You're such a fool, John. Can't you see it was done on purpose that way? If you had had such an alibi, and had given it to them at that moment, what a wonderful witness Taylor would have made. That alibi would have cleared you. Every question is a considered one, they are not fools. There is no hit and miss about their investigations, they were doing that *for* you, not against you."

"Well, I refused to tell them."

"Why, for God's sake. Why John?"

"It's true, I have got a personal matter to hide. It has nothing to do with Amanda's death. Nothing! And I'm damned if I'm going to let any tin pot policeman, probe into my private affairs. Everyone is entitled to their personal life. It should not be used as exhibit A, for police information. I'm damned if I'll let them use mine!"

"I'd hoped you would send for me, to tell me as a friend, privately, what all this was about. You're wrong, John. You're speaking of normal life and conditions. At this moment, your personal life *is* the field of police inquiry. Couldn't you possibly tell me what all this is? You must know I can be trusted and would be discreet. It'd give me the chance to clear you, off the record."

"No, Chris. You're becoming a policeman too, so confidence doesn't enter into it any longer."

Christopher Mainwaring drained his glass and stood up. "You're a stubborn bastard, John. You always were, even at school. I suppose it's that that helped you to stick out life with Amanda, the way you did. Well, I must go. It seems we can't help each other. I'm sorry."

John Gresham stood up with him. "I wonder if it will thicken suspicion around me, if I go away for a little? I'm feeling very tired, and sick of the sight of this house, and village."

"You must be very tired — with that coming from you, of all men."

"I think it's because it's mixed up with your detectives snooping around the place. They're always here, even at the Rectory fete."

"They have their job to do, and *you* must take it very seriously. But of course, go away. There's no curtailment of your liberty, though if possible, it'd be a good idea to leave your address with us. Nothing's been proved against you yet, and until it is, you're innocent. It'll do you good to go for a holiday. And while you're away, I do urge you to reconsider taking me into your confidence — it is of utmost importance to me." Chris looked squarely at John, to emphasise his last sentence.

John chose to disregard it. "The first thing I'll do is to go to London to consult my solicitor about all this. It looks as if he's going to have to brief some pretty good counsel. Wherever I end up after that, I'll send you my address."

"You won't be going out of country?"

John gave a short laugh at Chris's tone. "No Chris! I promise you, you won't have to bring in Interpol to find me!"

Chris put a hand on his shoulder. "This is no joking matter, John. Just don't be a blind stubborn fool. Use help when it's offered, I think you're unaware of how badly you need it. We've been friends for so many years, and all the time I have had enormous respect for you, and always will have. Not that that's much comfort to you just now. But if you change your mind, I'm still here, and would be glad to be your confidant. Meanwhile, have a good holiday, and I'll be hearing from you — your whereabouts, anyway."

*   *   *   *   *

As soon as Chris had gone, John sent for Taylor. "I'm going away for two or three weeks holiday, possibly into the country, I'm not sure yet. Would you pack a couple of suitcases for me, my dark suit, and the rest casual clothes. Oh, and some swimming gear, in case I go to the sea some of the time. I'll leave in my car for London as soon as the cases are packed, and set off for my holiday in a day or two from there."

"Will you be in touch with me, Sir, about your return?"

The anxiety and concern on Taylor's face, brought instant warmth through the ice surrounding John. "It's all right, old fellow. I'm not going to do anything stupid. I'm just taking a break from all this, that all. Then I'll be back again, to square up to it. I'll let you know where I am, when I know myself. I've assured the Chief Constable that I wouldn't be leaving the country."

Taylor heard his short dry laugh — he knew what that laugh meant. "It'll be all right in the end, Sir. We'll just have to give it more time."

"We have to believe that, don't we." John looked at him, and added, "it's great to have a chap like you around. Loyalty is at a high premium."

18. The police interview the Rector, again

Next morning while John Gresham was in London seeing his solicitor, Williams and Turner drove up Larmer village street to the Rectory. This morning, it was Nanny Bridget who opened the door to them.

"Sure, it's the two of you I'm wanting to see," was her direct frontal attack, in a rich Irish brogue. "What's all this I'm after hearing, about alibis for Mr John?"

"It would help his position, if he could mention anyone who'd been with him between the hours of 10 and 11:30, on the morning his wife disappeared," Williams said, with all the dignity he could muster, in the face of this blazing spitfire.

She flashed round on him. "All right so! I'm giving it even now, aren't I. He took Rufus for a walk, and came to see me, bless him!"

"At that time of day?"

"Sure an' it was — at a time, on that day. I'm telling you. He'd come back from London the evening before, I don't expect the poor lad remembers. He's got a lot on his mind just now."

"Why did he come to see you?"

"An' why wouldn't he? You be telling me that now. He likes to come, bless him. I helped to bring him up, along with his mother of course, God rest her soul — until he married that wife of his. Much good that did the poor boy! Sure, he often drops in for a bit of comfort, and a chat."

"In the middle of the morning?"

"Be Jeysus an' why not? Will you be telling me what time he ought to come, an' all?" she said in a biting tone.

Williams decided he didn't want to be clobbered by an infuriated Irish woman, so he didn't go any further into it. He just said, "well thank you for telling us. Now, may we see the Reverent Canon?"

When they were finally in the study with the Canon, Williams said, "I take it that Taylor has recently been along to see Nanny Bridget."

"Yes, he spent a couple of hours with her last evening. He often comes along and sees her, they were in the Gresham household together for many years, they're very good friends. I think they pretty well feel that they own Mr John." The Canon laughed happily.

"And Mr Gresham comes to see her too?"

"Oh often. She lives on it, from one visit to the next. Her life revolves round him."

"Would he come in the morning, say when he was taking his dog for a walk?" asked Williams.

"No, he'd never do that. He knows that she works in our house in the mornings, and he wouldn't dream of interrupting it. He drops in for a cup of tea with her in an afternoon, when he knows she's not busy then. Sometimes my wife and I join them, according to what we're doing. She even keeps his favourite fruitcake baked for him, ready in a tin. It's very nice to see them both. I think he often unburdens himself to her, and it gives her a purpose in her life."

"Would you know if he came here on the morning of the day his wife disappeared?"

"It's a long time ago to remember, Inspector. But I think it's highly unlikely. He may have come around that afternoon."

"I see, thank you Canon. Now I really came to see you on another matter. We're back to Jimmy, and what he told you when you questioned him."

"Oh yes?" A wary look crept across the Canon's face. This look appeared unfamiliar, and uncomfortable there. He sat down and looked at them both enquiringly.

"Without betraying the boy's confidences, we wonder whether you could give us the slightest lead out of what's he told you? That poor boy, is our key witness, so you can see how important this is, in getting to the bottom of this murder."

"What he told me has nothing to do with murder. Inspector, we have already discussed this, and I had nothing further to add to what I said then. I'm sorry." The Canon's tone was final.

"You see, Canon," Williams persisted, "you and I are really doing the same job, but we approach it from different angles. We're both out to protect and help humanity. Your approach is 'how can I give comfort and strength to human weakness?' Right?"

"Perfectly."

"Well, mine is 'whoever did this out of human weakness, must be found, so as to protect the rest of society.'"

"As I said before, Inspector, you must stick to your work, and I'll stick to mine."

Williams jaw hardened. He sat up in his chair aggressively. "Then I must tell you, unless I can get some co-operation from you — and I know you can give it — your friend John Gresham could be in deep trouble. Things don't look too good for him at the moment."

The Canon stood up and leant his elbow on the mantelpiece. He straightened up a yellow rose that was leaning out of the vase, and gazed intently for a long moment at the picture above his head, of that old country mansion. The silence ticked on, from the marble clock.

Williams broke in. He said quietly, and intently, "everything seems to converge on Beech Farm, in this case. First Jimmy was seen to be stumbling away from Beech Farm down the village street in the direction of the Manor. He was in a hurry."

"By whom?" snapped the Canon.

"By Wing Commander Cowper Sir," Turner said. "He was just setting out for his morning ride about 9:30 that morning. Later, the boy arrived at about the Manor in an excited state, and refused to leave until he had seen Mrs Gresham."

"He did see her."

"We know that," Williams said. "After hearing what he had to say, she set off in a fever of excitement, with her riding whip, but without her dogs. She too was in a hurry. Next she was seen walking up the village street, in the direction of Beech Farm."

"By Cowper again?"

"No Sir. This time by the barman," Turner said.

"Oh yes, he brought that chap here with him, when he came to Larmer."

"But even if he is a 'Foreigner', Canon, he can still see. You must understand, this has to be an 'eyes and ears' investigation. We can do no other," Williams said.

"Of course, we all fully understand that," the dry tone sounded strange, on the Canon's tongue.

"The third line bearing on Beech Farm, was John Gresham, only he was seen to be leaving it, through the hedge behind the copse. Again, at the operative time. He too will offer no explanation, not even to clear himself. So you see, Canon, it would appear that Beech Farm was the focal point, prior to, and doubtless at, the time of the murder. So now you can see how important it is to give us some lead, out of your talk with Jimmy. Even if only to clear your friends."

"I see it very clearly indeed," the Canon's voice was heavy with sadness.

"Why was Beech Farm, an unoccupied house, centre of this crime? Who was there to cause all these comings and goings? Why did John Gresham return from London suddenly, and totally unexpectedly, the previous afternoon? These are the answers we need. I believe, Canon, that you can give them to us." Williams never took his eyes off the Canon's face. He noted every flick of expression.

When he was blocked by a bar of silence from the Canon, he said: "so, you're not out to help humanity after all."

"Not in your way, Inspector."

"There's only one thing left for us now. We'll have to go and see the owner of the property at that time. Perhaps she could throw some light on who was trespassing, and why."

"Marion won't be able to help you," the Canon said quickly and vigorously. "She was a long way off at the time, in Nottingham."

"Was she?" Williams' question sounded innocent enough. "Well, perhaps you will decide to help us yourself, instead. Think it over, Canon — and its importance to your friend. But whether you help us or not, we shall finally ferret it out. Make no mistake about that. Even if it means ferreting it out in Court. I just thought you might prefer to volunteer it here in private, instead. We'll leave you now, but I do urge you to take this very seriously. You know where you can contact us at any time."

"Yes, of course. I do".

How ravaged the Canon's face had become. Williams found his thoughts jerking with pity, for this gentle, benign man, in spite of his obstinacy. But all the same, he suddenly shot at him: "Was John Gresham in Beech Farm grounds that morning?"

The Canon's face closed up.

"Your very silence, when you know how much is at stake for this man, could be an indictment against him."

"No, no, Inspector! I do assure you, it must not be read as that. I beg of you to be fair to him!"

Williams had to snap his mind away from compassion for this old man, at the honest struggle he was going through. "It's you who are not being fair to him. It's a matter of choice, but I'd have thought your greater loyalty would be to him, rather than to that boy Jimmy."

"Everyone is equal in God's eyes."

"Well, I'm prepared to make you an offer, Canon. You must interview that boy Jimmy, here in my presence. I will give you the questions to ask him, and I rely on you to interpret his answers correctly. Otherwise you will undoubtedly be taken as a key witness to Court." Williams voice had a sharp edge to it. The Canon walked to the window, and stood in silence for a long time, as if communing with his own personal God.

Williams voice cut through the silent room like a bullet. "You are under an obligation to do this, in the interests of Justice."

At last, the Canon said in a wavering voice, "I have to agree to that, I can do no other." His eyes held dark suffering. He had suddenly become an old man.

"Thank you. Just let me know when you can arrange it." Williams tone had become gentler.

Then the Canon unexpectedly straightened up his shoulders. He faced Williams squarely, and with great dignity said, "I do know that John Gresham could never have committed such a crime. Just as you will spare nobody to prove his guilt, so I will spare nobody to prove his innocence."

"That's fine. That's what we're asking you to do."

"Please, I must ask you to leave now. I find this overwhelmingly distressing." That last spark of spirit seemed to have exhausted him.

*   *   *   *   *

Williams' thoughts flew along the road, as the police car soared over the hills, with Turner driving it in grim silence.

Then Williams said, "so, by crucifying this old man, we'll get to the truth."

"Well, that's one way of putting it," Turner said through his teeth.

"Frank, he knows perfectly well what happened at Beech Farm, or he is making a pretty accurate guess as to what his lambs were up to."

"We'll wait for his call. It'd be easier for him, if you saw him alone with the boy."

"Okay, if that's how you feel about it. After that, we go north to see Marion Ferguson, though I know the heart of it all, lies here."

19. Life is so complicated

After seeing his solicitor, John had lunch at his club, and then returned to his Mayfair apartment. No sooner had he got in and the phone rang. It was Richard Pendleton.

"Good, I hoped I'd catch you in, John. Are you busy at the moment? Could you spare me the time if I pop round to have a word with you?"

"So, you've joined the witch-hunt too. Yes, come around by all means. After all, the rest of your Force seems to have been wasting their time 'having a word' with me. There's nothing to stop you joining in."

"You poor old boy! You've really got it badly, haven't you. I wouldn't be bothering you, but this is important..."

"That's what they all say," John broke in.

"It's about Amanda's jewellery."

"Her what?"

"Her jewellery. I can't tell you more on the phone. I'll come straight round."

*   *   *   *   *

Richard settled into a deep armchair, and looked round him. He said with a sigh of comfort: "This is a really lovely apartment, isn't it." He thought it must be worth a mint.

"It's Amanda's apartment, she'd bought it with her money," John was quick to say.

"Don't be so touchy, old chap. You must know that I didn't mean that. I was thinking only in terms of the comfort of it, in the middle of a busy frustrating day."

"All the same, I think I shall probably sell it. It's too pretentious for me, I'd prefer something simpler. But tell me, what's all this about Amanda's jewellery?"

"She had some pretty valuable staff, didn't she?"

"She did. Among other things, she had a beautiful necklace of diamonds and drop emeralds, with a matching bracelet, and pendant earrings. They were very lovely, and looked superb on her. It was an engagement present from her father. He'd died by the time we got married. It was almost as if he knew."

"Where are they now?" asked Richard.

"D'you know, I've no idea. Never thought of looking. I imagine they must be in their place."

"And where's that?"

"In the wall safe in her bedroom. I had it fitted for her security."

"Was it exposed?"

"No, there was a Regency gilt mirror hung over the front of it."

"Did anyone else know it was there?"

"No, unless Mrs Clark did. I never thought of that."

"Can you remember what other valuable pieces she had?" asked Richard.

"Yes, she had a two-tier string, and a single string, of real pearls. One had been her mother's, the other a present from her overindulgent father on her 17th birthday — that was the one found on her. They were wonderful pearls, beautifully graded, pretty near priceless."

"Anything else?"

"There were some valuable rings, one particularly so with a square cut emerald. It was a favourite of hers. She liked emeralds, they suited her colouring. She also had some valuable bracelets, I remember a lovely sapphire one, set in chip diamonds, and a necklace of opals set in diamonds. Various clips and brooches. The best of her brooches was the one I gave her. It was my wedding present to her. It was a long spray, made of solitaire diamonds, set in platinum — they were good carat diamonds. For your information Richard, it was my money which paid for this. I sold one of the family pictures, a Landseer."

"Of course, it never occurred to me to think otherwise."

"She had a lovely ruby pendant, and matching earrings, but she hardly ever wore them. Nothing was ever imitation, if Amanda was to wear it," said John.

He swung round to Richard. "I did love her very greatly when we married, whatever the press are pleased to say now, or the police to think. The first year was deeply happy — for both of us. Then her illness started after she had miscarried our first child. Gradually, she became like a child herself — to be looked after. But she was a naughty, wilful, querulous child. Our life together became just a... passing of years. I wonder can you understand any of this?"

Richard nodded, more moved that he'd care to admit. "All of it, old chap. But it's nothing to do with the relationship between you, that I'm bothered about. I've come about her jewellery, whether it is all still there, and intact."

"They think among other things, that I've swiped her jewellery, do they?"

"Oh, don't be a fool, John. You really must get this chip off your shoulder."

"Your chaps put it there," said John.

"I'm not bothered about their end — that's their job. It up here that's my pigeon. Now John, think back, does the name Arnold Braithwaite mean anything to you?"

"Certainly it does! Everyone knows he was Amanda's boyfriend, and a great friend of Ashley Wentworth, Amanda's brother. Ashley let Amanda and Arnold use his apartment for their liaison. Arnold was a very smooth operator."

"I think that too, every reason to. Right now, he's at the treatment centre, for withdrawal from hard drugs — heroin in his case. He started on it four months ago, after Amanda went missing."

"As fond of her as that, was he!"

"Or as angry as that! I'm not sure yet."

"He'd been staying with Amanda at Larmer for a few days, in fact immediately prior to her disappearance. He scarpered only minutes before I got back."

"How do you know this?" Richard sat bolt upright.

"Taylor told me, that same evening."

"Have you looked at her jewellery since?" Richard asked sharply.

"No, it never occurred to me to do so."

"Well, I think we'd better do so, straight away."

"Why?"

We have the knowledge, but not quite enough evidence, that Arnold Braithwaite is a jewel thief — and in a big way too."

"God Almighty!"

"Goes further than that. He was found to be very ill, suffering from untreated withdrawal — what the drug people would call 'cold turkey'. His was a particularly severe one. The man whose apartment he found it in, at Eaton Place no less, is a jewel craftsman by the name of Quincey. He designs and makes up jewellery for top London jewellers. He could even have made up that diamonds spray, you gave Amanda. It's our guess, though we haven't yet enough evidence, that he breaks it up too. His other side line, is making near perfect imitations, so good that they are sold by top flight jewellers. John, you see it's all beginning to tie up."

"What chance led you to it?"

"We've suspected Arnold Braithwaite for some time. But we've not found him associated with any receiver before. But when he went on to heroin, that led us to Quincey. Of course, now he's a dead loss to that character."

"What made you suspect Arnold Braithwaite, in the first place?"

"As you know, he was a well-connected unattached male, of the sort that hostesses fall over themselves to collect, to partner their unattached women guests. He was seen at many London society functions. When there have been jewellery robberies, we keep our eyes on the lists of guests. A common denominator comes out of this, that may give us a lead. Many of the thefts are done from inside. For the last few years, wherever jewels of real value have been stolen, Arnold Braithwaite had usually been a house guest, or a guest at a particular function, where the jewels had been worn. Our attention was focused on this man. He was the common denominator. But in the last four months, just as we were getting him taped, he hasn't shown up. Neither have there been any big robberies of note. Then a stroke of luck! He was found desperately ill, by the drug doctor, in Quincey's Eaton Place apartment — Quincey, a jewel craftsman!"

"But that's only suspicion. I must say, you people seen to take a lot on yourselves, on the grounds of only suspicion."

"Oh no. We've usually got circumstantial evidence too. But as you know, a good detective is like a good priest, he can look the chap in the eye, and have a pretty good idea if he's lying."

"You must be joking!" John said bitterly.

Richard ignored this, and went on: "Perhaps Amanda knew nothing about that side of this Gent... or did she?"

"Of course she didn't! She didn't need money."

"No, not money. But she was the sort of person who'd join in any crazy game for kicks — the more outrageous and dangerous, the better. Or perhaps, she'd never knew about that part of Arnold Braithwaite's life, up until that last visit of his to Larmer."

"Taylor did say they had had an almighty row, but then there was nothing new for Amanda. He skived off in the middle of the row. It may have been nothing to do with guessing that I was on my way home, after all," John said slowly.

"It may have had something to do with a pocket full of jewellery, or perhaps being caught in the act of collecting a pocket full. But you can see now, why I should so suddenly be interested in the whereabouts of her jewellery. I suppose it was insured?"

"Yes, heavily."

"And Amanda wasn't short of cash in any way? I mean, she wouldn't need to collect the insurance, knowing full well the boyfriend had the goods in his possession?" asked Richard.

"I wouldn't know the machinations of her mind. I couldn't even hazard a guess. As for the state of her money, I'm not aware of her ever being short. But you'd have to find all that out, from her bank and stockbroker."

"I'm jumping the gun right now. First, we've got to look in that safe, and see exactly what it contains. If there's anything missing, then we can start working on Arnold Braithwaite, in the treatment centre."

"I can even find it in my heart to be sorry for the poor bastard," John said with feeling. "So there goes another suspect, but with a different motive."

"Precisely! Could even be the cause of Arnold going on to heroin, an escape route that he needed."

John slipped one of the keys off the ring and handed it to Richard. "This is my key to the safe, Amanda had the only other one. I haven't a clue where hers is. But will you yourself go down to Larmer, and open the safe, and see what the situation is? I'll just write combination down for you. If you find any jewellery in it, put it into your own custody at the bank, until I get back."

"Get back? Where from?"

"I haven't decided yet. It'll be somewhere in this country. I'm getting so browned off with all this, it's getting me down. I'm going away for a while, for a break."

"I don't blame you. Leave it all with me, I'll take charge of the whole thing." Richard leant back in his chair, deep in thought, and then said, "you know John, there would almost have be a woman somewhere in this jewel game. If it wasn't Amanda, then we have to look elsewhere... for a woman equally sociable, and well connected."

"But why a woman?" asked John.

"Because of the kind of drill. Let's pretend for the sake of simplicity, that woman is Amanda. There are two ways she can operate. She can swap her emeralds, for her friend Belinda's diamonds for an evening function. They do the swap during the day. As soon as Amanda has her friend's diamonds, she gets them smartly along to Quincey. He takes photos of them, and gets them back to Amanda in time for her to wear at the function. By lunchtime next day, Quincey has the replica made. He gives the replica to Amanda, who hands over to him the real thing. She then gives the replica back to her friend Belinda, and retrieves her own emeralds. Meanwhile, Quincey is busy breaking up the real diamond necklace, now in his possession."

"But do women swap jewels? It seems extraordinarily irresponsible of them, if they do."

"You'd be surprised. Some do anything for vanity. These women do exist, John."

"What a risk to take," said John.

"The second ploy doesn't involve a swap at all, it's just straightforward 'borrowing' of a piece of jewellery from a wealthy easy friend, for an evening occasion. You could imagine one of Amanda's girlfriends in a generous mood, perhaps after smoking pot, saying 'yes, you can borrow it for tonight if you like. I won't be using it'. Then the same deal with Quincey follows. These replicas are beautifully made. That's why many of the thefts by that method, are never discovered until quite a lot later."

"I'd wonder they're ever discovered. Because most women don't know a great deal about that kind of thing."

"I imagine many never are. But the owner of a valuable necklace learns to know a fair amount about it. It may be that she notices the clasp fits a bit differently from what she is used to. Or the pearls don't feel quite the same as she rubs them against her cheek. Perhaps the setting of a stone slants slightly differently, and no longer catches the light. It's often the tiniest detail, that gives the game away," Richard explained.

"Where does Arnold come in on this?"

"His job is to spot the pieces worth swiping, at the various functions that he's invited to, and then to notify Quincey and Amanda. He does the fetching and carrying, and if the 'borrowing' technique isn't practical, then he does the out and out theft instead. It's my guess, that he's a pretty practised hand at it by now. You see, no craftsman could make a perfect copy, without having the original piece in front of him, even for a few hours — especially when the copy is the supreme standard of work, that Quincey turns out."

"And I suppose I could be a member of this club. As an MP, I get invited to a number of country houses, where rich people hang out," John laughed.

"And that's not just the joke that it sounds. It is in fact, one of the recognised methods. I won't mention any names," Richard's voice was quite firm.

"Richard, from what I've seen, I wouldn't be doing your job for anything on earth."

"Quite right, it'd be no good your applying for it! Well, have a good holiday, I'll see you when you get back."

As John closed the front door, his face was furrowed with concern. Richard hadn't volunteered a word about the suspicion in Larmer concerning himself, and wouldn't even rise when he alluded to it. You'd never be able to tell what Richard knew, or how much. He'd been in love with Marion for years. Some men develop a sixth sense about the women they love.

*   *   *   *   *

Cornwall must have been at the back of his mind all along really, he thought, as he drove along the Great West Road. The Greater London suburbs were thinning out now. It was a bit late in the afternoon to be setting off, but ever since Coverack had crystallised in his mind an hour ago, he was impatient to get going. He rang the hotel first, to see if they had a room, and booked one overlooking the sea. It would be a good idea to spend a night at Winchester, before driving down there.

He had spent a couple of holidays in Coverack, with Colonel Ferguson and Marion. It had been an oasis in the midst of his difficulties, and the mere thought of it had been his mental refuge, ever since. Now it would be again.

*   *   *   *   *

His memory shot back to that election period. The way he had been swept along in the keenness and thrust of political battle, and Marion who was swept along too, beside him. She was there every moment, ready to shoulder every job he piled onto her. But she had a sweet sanity, that he entirely relied upon, and she was as keen as himself.

He had not known her until then. He had always seen her as 'Colonel Ferguson's nice young daughter' at Beech Farm, where she grew up. But the generation gap of 11 years between them, had put her outside his own horizon.

It was only when the election was over, and he had won his seat with the help of her efforts, that this vacuum opened up beside him. He'd never envisage missing anyone so much. He found himself wandering up to Beech Farm at weekends, quite unnecessarily, to keep her informed of the latest debates and constituency problems. On Saturday mornings he would sit in the party constituency rooms in Salisbury, so that any of his constituents could speak to him personally about their difficulties, or suggestions. Then he found himself asking her if she'd like to come along, and help. Her eyes were alight as she accepted, big eyes, the colour of violets. Saturdays became the pivot of his week.

He soon fell into the habit of taking her out to lunch, after their Saturday morning at the constituency office had finished. Later they prolonged it, by stopping the car on the drive back to Larmer, for a walk over the Downs. She was a rare kind of girl, you didn't have to keep talking to, and one of the few who made no demands. Their silences were complete contentment. So this was how peace felt — a new experience for him.

Then one day, while he was sitting in the House as an MP listening to a debate, his thoughts strayed to wondering what she was doing at that moment. It shook him, as his thoughts tumbled about. But by the time that the House rose, he knew how unfair that was. She was young, with all her future before her, and what had he, a married man, got to offer. He must keep out of her way.

He stayed in London for the whole of the next month, and delegated a deputy to do his Saturday mornings at the constituency office in Salisbury. Then, when Amanda got at too close quarters in the London apartment, there wasn't enough space to dodge her moods and querulousness. So, one weekend, he escaped to Larmer for a breather, having first made up his mind that he would not go near Beech Farm.

But he had not reckoned with the village grapevine, relaying news of his arrival within minutes. About five o'clock on a Saturday afternoon, Taylor showed Marion into the library, when he was deep in government reports. Because he had been caught off guard, he was gruff and unwelcoming with her. He must have a boorish sort of oaf, he thought.

She seemed not to notice as she said, "I've brought you all the reports of the Saturday morning constituency surgery sessions. As you don't come now, I thought I'd better save them up until you come again. Then you'll know what's going on in the constituency." She no longer looked squarely at him, in her direct way. A shy kind of confusion seemed to have robbed her of that precise spontaneity of hers.

"Thank you for taking such trouble. I'll go over them," he had not meant to sound as curt as that.

"John," she looked straight at him now. "Why aren't you coming to Salisbury any more on Saturdays. What's happened?"

"I'm so busy," he said abruptly. He sounded rather surly.

"Surely not busier then you were at the start? Have I... in any way put my foot in it, somehow? Have I?"

Her humility! He couldn't stand humility from such as her. He stood looking out the window, with his back to her, struggling to find the right answer.

Still with his back to her, he said stiffly, "you mustn't blame yourself, Marion. It has nothing to do with you."

He heard her quiet voice for the middle of the room, "What has it to do with, then? Whatever it is, won't you come back? We need you."

He couldn't stop himself. Without a word, he strode across the room and folded her close against him. He closed his eyes with the relief of it. The whole world took on a different dimension.

And later they walked — walked miles over the downs, glorying in their own countryside, and each other. The full impact of the misery it would bring, had not hit them then. They could only think of the wonder of a love given, and a love returned.

*   *   *   *   *

It was a few weeks after this that he told Colonel Ferguson when he was playing chess with him, at Beech Farm. They were in the habit of playing this game together, quite frequently. Sometimes Marion would sit the other side by the fire, but this night she had a heavy cold, and left them early.

John suddenly blurted out: "I've got something to tell you, Sir."

"I'd rather wondered when you would," the Colonel said calmly.

"You know then... about Marion and me? Did she tell you?"

"No John. But Marion and I are quite close. You don't think something like this could happen to her, without my knowing, do you?"

"It happened of itself, you know."

"It does," the Colonel said quietly.

"It's not fair on her. I wish it hadn't."

"So do I. But there's no escaping the fact, so you both have to be practical over it."

"You see, I so want to marry her, but I can't while I'm married to Amanda. In her state of health, Amanda has nobody but me to look after her."

"I realise that. Don't think, dear boy, that I haven't given a great deal of thought to this."

"Marion too understands this perfectly. It's tremendous the way she just accepts it."

"She would of course. But that doesn't stop her from getting badly hurt."

"What can we do?"

"I suppose it wouldn't be possible to pack in the whole thing, make a clean break? As humanly as possible I mean?"

"What do you think?" said John.

"No, I suppose not. It could even kill her as a person, she'd wilt like a cut flower. And it's *her* happiness I'm thinking of, solely that. She's already edgy with frustration. I see her come down in the mornings, after another night of not enough sleep. It isn't good John."

"Tell me what to do, Colonel."

"I'll leave it in your hands. Make her happy, John. I don't care what you do, so long as you make her happy, and take great care of her." He sighed before adding, "if this had to happen, then thank God it's you. The irony of it is, there's no man I would have preferred more, as a son-in-law. I'd always hoped it'd be someone like you, when it came... but not in these circumstances."

"I'll take the very greatest care of her. Apart from my duty to Amanda, she will always be my first consideration. The wretched thing is, there's nothing I could want more, than to be your son-in-law. But thank you for your trust."

The old man got up and poured them each out a brandy. They sat over the fire, watching the glowing logs.

The Colonel suddenly said, "I'd like you to come away on holiday with Marion and I. We go to a lovely spot in the southwest corner of the Cornish coast, called Coverack. It would be such a happy thing for her, and make it easier. We could go next month, April is a lovely time there, a paradise of Narcissus."

*   *   *   *   *

At first, he couldn't bring himself to go to her, he never understood why. Then came the morning he woke to find the place blanked out in a thick sea fog, as only that corner of Cornwall can be.

In the afternoon he walked with her along the top of the cliffs. They were just able to see the path ahead of them. They sat in the heather, on a jutting piece of cliff, and listened to the foghorn of the Lizard Lighthouse, warning the shipping off the rocks, in deep moaning tones. The ships replied, with higher anxious notes. The fog spangled her fair hair with dew drops. The sea was calm, with an idle lapping of waves against the rocks below.

"I love this," she said. "It blindfolds the rest of the world, makes an isolated island for us."

"I'll bet they don't in those ships out there," he laughed. It was absolute solitude. He kissed her, the way he wanted to, and he could feel her response, and they became part of the wilderness.

That night she said, "I'm frightened of it, John. Be gentle with me." He had been gentle with her. He could feel her love reaching out to him, and breaking through her nervousness. It was then she gave him the fullness of reward.

*   *   *   *   *

The Colonel went away for a few days afterward — to see an old army friend living in Falmouth, he said. He sensed everything that happened to that girl. In the next three weeks, her love matured into a rich passionate response. This truly was their honeymoon. They would watch the swinging beams of the lighthouse, as they swept across. She became part of the luminous nights, part of the vivid days. Together, they shared the perfect rhythm of happiness, in the place, the time, and each other.

When they returned to Larmer, they started to use the summer house in Beech Farm Copse. It was absolute privacy. Their love, generated by their minds and their hearts, was a completion. They shared all their thoughts, their whole lives, in that summer house.

The next year, the three of them went away again to Coverack. The old Colonel gave them his blessing all the time. It was such great personal grief to him when the Colonel died the year after that — he had truly grown to love him.

*　　*　　*　　*　　*

He understood why she had to leave Larmer, after her father's death — to make a new life for herself. He could offer her no hope of marriage, Amanda was physically a healthy woman. He could only give her his absolute love. But now that only seemed to make her suffer. For him, the pain of her absence when it came, grew to be nearly unendurable.

The short notes she occasionally sent at first, had to suffice. He found himself watching for the post. But what had happened since then? In the past few months there had been not a word from her — not a word.

Perhaps she was making out successfully after all. In which case it would be totally wrong to disturb her. Perhaps she had learned to love someone else — perhaps. And his own need of her in those last four months, could never be described.

Sometimes, when he reached an all-time low, he would close his eyes and imagine her suddenly coming through

250

the door, as she had done before, breathing life into him again, with her love.

After this sort of euphoria, he would go out and take Rufus his dog, for a good sharp walk over the Downs, to steady himself. Dreaming and mooning were no good, they just made a chap sag at the seams. He felt like a flat earthling, caught in the spiral of fate. The peace of Coverack would help him now, he felt sure of that.

<u>20. Marion's holiday</u>

Marion sat on a rock by the beach in Coverack, resting her chin on her hand, as she watched the incoming tide. It was sliding slowly into the rock pools, with seaweed swaying as the waves receded. It was late afternoon. The place was as perfect as ever, just the wind, the sea, the heather-covered cliffs, and the gulls wheeling off the headland.

She had been here nearly a month now, and it had done everything for her. The doctor had been right. To be completely cut off from the rest of life like this, had been just what she needed. She had carried out his instructions exactly. She had not seen a newspaper, or watched television for so long, or even had her post forwarded, so that she had stopped wondering what was going on in the world. None of it mattered any more.

Her sleep at nights was long and deep, without the help of any pills. It was glorious to lie in bed, lulled by the sound and hiss of the waves, and to watch the Lizard Lighthouse fan its light over the sea. Shipping would glow on the horizon. Next thing she would know, it would be morning.

She was eating well, and as for Dinah, she was starting to get a bit fat.

As she watched the rock shadows lengthen, she said aloud to Dinah lying beside her, "I'm drinking all of this in, Dinah–girl, storing it up to remember next winter, when we're in the dreary industrial north."

Dinah stood up, stretched, and gave a huge yawn, then moved cautiously across the rock to Marion's other side, quietly edging her further away from its centre, which was smooth and flat. Having taken possession of the centre herself, she flopped down again beside Marion, shook a sand-fly off her head, and promptly went into another doze. She had moved as if she had glue on her paws. She hated the way her paws slithered on these rocks, but it was preferable to the sandy beach. There, her head was too near the ground, and every time she moved, her short legs scuffed sand into her eyes. She was prepared to sit on Marion's towel when she went in for a swim, but that was as far as she'd go.

After a while Marion said to her, "but why should we live in a city in the North, Dinah-girl? It's a bit silly, isn't it. We're country people, and used to village life in the South. Why should we stick it out in a city?"

Yes. Why shouldn't she buy a cottage here, and settle down in *this* village? It had the advantage of being almost as far from Larmer as Nottingham was. Fisherman's cottages did come up for sale now and then, she'd seen them. Dinah gave another jaw-cracking yawn.

Marion laughed down at her, gently grasped her long thin nose, and shook it. "You're a funny girl," she said, "You understand everything I say, even what I'm thinking, you don't need the words. Even when I'm correcting books, and I'm too busy to bother with you till I've finished, look how you slink away, and reproach me with those brown eyes, and I haven't uttered a word about it. You've got the gist of what I'm thinking at the moment, haven't you?"

No. There'd be no university job down here. Exeter was the nearest, and that was miles away. It would mean going back to school teaching. There'd be plenty of school jobs to be had in a place like Helston. That was only 10 miles away, on a good main road. The job wouldn't be so good, but it might be worth the swap.

Dinah flopped her nose across Marion's lap, wide open eyes fixed on her, her ears twitching against the sand-flies, waiting for what came next.

"It's more fun in a place like this, where everybody joins in, isn't it Dinah. We'd have more friends than we are used to. I don't have to spell that out for you, do I. And we've known it here for so long, it's like a second Larmer to us."

There'd be Christmas here too, a real Christmas. Perhaps they have carol singing too. She already knew about daffodils. Dinah's eyes grew wise and wistful.

Marion sat and dreamed. This sudden idea seemed to be the answer to her problem. She'd drive into Helston in the morning and see a local estate agent. That modern Scandinavian furniture would look a bit odd inside those whitewashed cottage walls, or would it? She could grow her own vegetables, and salads and flowers, in the cottage garden. Maybe there'd be an apple or a plum tree, in it too. She could get manure, and eggs and butter and milk, from one of the farms. Go out with the fishermen and catch some of her own fish. She could help with the church flowers, do a bit of riding. That picture of a life she felt at home in, was rising vividly before her eyes.

And strangely, now she could think of Larmer again. She even felt at peace, as her thoughts reached back to it. The desperate need to shut it out, had gone. She was picturing those grassy battlements of the Downs. The view from the summit of Win Green near the Dorset border, commanding four counties, and across to the sea, even to the Isle of Wight. The valleys sloping steeply away, would be yellow with ragwort at this time of year, with butterflies flopping lazily in and out. There, a pale sun was held by the morning mists, which later melted in the warmth of a purring September day, like this.

She could almost hear the shiver of leaves on the beech trees round her old home, and the cawing of rooks, as they jostled in the treetops. She could hear Old Tom's unhurried heavy tread across the yard, as he went towards the kitchen garden, where probably the ghost of the Little Grey Lady would still be flitting among the fruit trees. Did she miss her? Did she know she'd left? She could almost hear again, the banging of the tool shed door in the wind. Old Tom so often left it open. And the way the house settled down to its own muffled sounds at night, after she had gone to bed. Petals falling from the flower vases, the creak of oak floors, fire embers falling in on themselves, and the whirring before the striking of the grandfather clock in the hall.

There would be brilliant asters in bloom now, and heavy headed dahlias, and sheaves of sunflowers. The trees at this moment, would be making elongated shadows on the gold-green grass, just before the sun went down. And later, those white mists would wrap the village for the night.

Dinah, who had contentedly slipped into another doze, suddenly lifted her head. She gave a sharp bark, and stood up. She was looking towards the cliff path, her ears pricked, and her nose twitching. She started making a quiet whining sound and was shivering with excitement.

"Don't be silly, Dinah. Sit down! It's not time to go in yet. That'll only be people from the hotel walking down to the beach. You needn't start pretending to be interested, after the way you snub anyone who dares to admire you. You with your toffee-nosed manner! But you can't help it, can you. All your breed are alike. You just latch on to your own family, and give them all you've got, don't you, Dinal-girl." And Marion pulled her back on her lap, to cuddle her.

Though this usually was all Dinah asked of life, now she wriggled free, took up her position as before, and stood watching the cliff path. Then suddenly, with tremendous barking, she shot away, slipping over the rocks in her haste, and tore up the cliff path, barking all the way.

In astonishment, Marion stood up, to see what all this was about. Near the top of the path, she saw Dinah run towards a tall man who had just come into view. There she was jumping up at him, with those excited sharp barks. Such a noise and a fuss. Then she was astonished to see the man bend down, and fussed Dinah. "Little Dinah! Whatever are you doing? Where's your mistress then?" she called.

Marians feet froze to the beach. The world around her shivered. "God, it's John," she gasped.

21.   A meeting in Cornwall

John saw Marion standing on the beach, as Dinah barking ecstatically, ran to her side. He saw the blank look of horror on her face, as he drew near. Her lips had fallen apart, a look of bewilderment had come into her eyes. Even though their meeting was totally unexpected, surely it shouldn't have had this effect of her.

He could think of nothing to say, so he found himself saying trite things. "Well, what a surprise! Fancy Dinah remembering me like that. What a welcome from her."

She said almost pleadingly, "why have you come, John?"

"As bad as that, is it? I came for a rest, and a holiday. I came to the place where I had been completely happy — I thought it might help me, as it did before. And you?"

"Me too — the same."

"When did you arrive?"

"Four weeks ago. I'll be here for another three weeks."

"That's a longish holiday, isn't it?" These polite formalities with a stranger called Marion were getting him down.

"I haven't been well," said Marion. "The doctor ordered me to get right away from everything, for as long as I could."

"Such as what?"

"Work, letters, newspapers, time and purpose. He said I was to float in limbo land. I've been doing just that — I could here."

He looked at her intently. "You've not even seen a paper?"

"No. Nor opened a letter. Not for four glorious weeks. I'd no idea how restful it could be."

"So you've no idea what's going on in the world?"

"None. And I don't want to know yet."

Can you bear it, he wondered. Aloud, he said, "I'm sorry, I didn't know you'd been ill."

She looked away from him. He saw the quick birdlike turn of her head, that he remembered so well.

"I'm all right now. The doctors said I had been overdoing it a bit, my batteries needed recharging. I'm cured now. It's this place that's done it," she said jerkily.

"It's that damned university job you're doing. Working far too hard at it, I'll bet. I remember in the election campaign, what a glutton you were for work."

The anxious concern in his voice softened her stiff stance for a moment. He was quick to notice it.

"Marion, couldn't we sit down here for a minute? You don't have to talk. Let's just sit together quietly for a while. It's been a long time. This is a shock to both of us. It's so good to see you."

Dinah sat down too, between them, utterly content. She stretched forwards, resting her long thin nose on her front paws, keeping her eyes on both of them. John stroked her head, and her long smooth back. "She's shaped into a lovely little dog, hasn't she? I'd no idea she'd turn out as well as this, when I gave her to you, even though she was the best pup in the litter. How long ago was that? Three years?"

"Four," she said abruptly.

"She pricks her ears beautifully, so evenly. She's really a showpiece now — but too much of a pet for that, I guess."

Dinah twitched one ear. She knew perfectly well she was being talked about, and admired. John went on stroking her, while Marion sat staring fixedly ahead.

At last he said, "Marion, would you look at me for a moment?"

She took a deep breath, and then turned her head reluctantly, and met his eyes squarely. He looked at her gently, her violet eyes were open very wide.

He said, "if you don't want me here, and would rather I left, I'll go first thing in the morning. I had no idea you'd be here, you must believe that."

She nodded.

He went on, "I don't want to intrude on you. You haven't answered any of my letters since... we last met. I could only assume that you didn't want me to go on writing, so that's why I've stopped. I don't know what all this is about. I must say, at no time did it ever occur to me, that you'd be so reluctant to see me, not after all the things we've shared for so long. But I'll go in the morning, if that's what you wish. You must tell me what you want me to do."

She could see the lines on his face, that spoke of a great misery of spirit, and weariness — and a dark pain in his eyes. She covered his hand that was stroking Dinah, with her own. She clung to his fingers. "John, don't go. I'm sorry. I'm sorry. It was the shock, I think."

He picked up her hand, turned it over slowly, and kissed its palm. He looked up at her then, with a quiet smile. "Don't worry my angel. It's all right. We'll take it slowly and gently, while we find one another again, and perhaps at last, unwind. If at any moment you want me gone, just say so." She was crying unashamedly now, as peace stole over her. Dinah started whimpering, she jumped into her lap, and started licking her face.

"She'll be all right, Dinah, don't worry. I think this is what that mistress of yours needs, just now," said John.

Marion smiled through her tears, trying to dodge her face away from Dinah's darting tongue. John handed her his handkerchief. "That's to wipe off the licks, as well as your tears." He laughed softly at her.

"I don't know what I'd have done without her, John."

"I know. It's been a relief to me that you had her. I guessed you two would feel like that." He pulled her to her feet. "Let's go to the hotel now and get ready for dinner. I'll meet you in the bar beforehand, say in an hour?"

She nodded.

"So, we'll be happy, Marion?"

She looked up swiftly. How tall he was. Just the same striking looking man. His mouth had a gentle expression he kept for her — it had haunted her all these months. Others saw only tautness of his jaw. It was another world when he came.

She laughed softly, and again nodded.

*   *   *   *   *

It had been an evening of celebration. She had never known John as happy as this. His whole face was radiant with an intensity of joy. At this moment, he looked nearer 25 than 35. She had forgotten how real happiness felt. Yet soon after 10 o'clock, she suddenly felt exhausted. He was quick to spot it.

"Would you would like to slip off to bed, my darling? You look ready to flake out."

"Would you mind?"

"Of course not. It's all this sudden excitement on top of your illness. I'll see you upstairs to your room, and then go for a night walk over the Headland. D'you remember how we used to watch the stars from there?"

"We will again," she said.

He stood up and took her arm in a protective way. "Come on, Dinah!"

Dinah was running in circles round the two of them, and then jumping her paws up and down excitedly. John scooped her up, and then handed her to Marion. "I can see just what sort of a spoilt girl she has been turned into," he laughed.

He took Marion to her bedroom door and kissed her cheek. "Goodnight my darling, sleep very well. It's meant everything to me to find you here, you will never know how much. See you at breakfast." He turned away quickly, and went downstairs.

Inside the bedroom, in the darkness, Marion leant her head against the closed door. She shut her eyes. She could hear the waves slap and hiss, against the cliffs. The wind was getting up. She could picture him striding over the headland, stopping to smell the wind and sea, and telling the stars of his need for her.

But it was no good — no good! She longed for him too, never more than at this moment. But if she allowed herself to start that again, she knew that this time, she could never break away. And now, above everything else, she *had* to break away... what else could she do?"

Dinah's whimpering broke through her thoughts. Her front paws were on the bed, and she was wagging her tail, demanding attention. "All right, you old nuisance," Marion sighed. She switched on the light, and lifted Dinah onto the bed. She swallowed two sleeping pills, the first time she had even thought of them for four weeks. She slowly and absently, got ready for bed.

*　　*　　*　　*　　*

"So, we'll be happy, Marion?" John had said yesterday.

But next morning, John could see how wrong he'd been. She had developed a thin-lipped reserve about her. To an outsider, she appeared happy and smiling, but to him, he could see clearly the forced effort it was, he knew her so well. He was completely mystified.

The sun was shining, with the promise of another golden day. Gulls were swooping off the headland with desolate cries.

"Shall we bathe this morning?" he suggested.

"We could," she said uncertainly. "But its low tide at 11, so it'd be better after lunch."

"Well, shall we drive over to Helford instead, and walk along the estuary, then call in at the Wainwright's Arms for a beer?"

"Yes, the walk would do Dinah good."

He shot her a quick look. Her tone had been the polite and distant one, used for strangers on a bus. He swallowed, let it pass, and led the way out to his car.

As the day went on, she built an aloof, impersonal barrier between them. It became a solid wall round her. But the next day, she had moments of lowering it, as if her love had broken through, in spite of herself. Then she became the warm and glowing girl he knew. There was no denying the existence of her love. He could see it creep into her eyes at unguarded moments, he seemed to spend much of his time watching for it. Yet after one of these intervals, the barrier would not only go up, but be reinforced.

These alternating moods went on for several days. John never knew which one he was in for next — the glowing or the stringent. She even invited other hotel guests to join them in what they planned to do — people he knew that she was not in the least interested in. She was using them as a shield. A shield against what? Surely not against him. She only had to tell him to go, and she knew he would do so immediately. But she didn't tell him that, or even imply it. In an offhand way, she seemed to cling to him.

He longed to help her in the obvious muddle, and struggle, she was going through. But it seemed as if he was the one person in the universe who could not do so. He felt at a loss, and deeply worried. It made his own problem slither into a distant background.

He never once mentioned Amanda's death. As she had been cast off from all news, he decided it was far better for her, to remain in ignorance and peace. She must have been pretty ill. Perhaps these moods were a by-product of her illness. But he found it difficult not to discuss his own troubles with her.

He never attempted to express his love to her. He was too sure she would recoil from him, and that he could not stand. Sometimes, as they sat on the heather on the cliff tops, and he watched her sitting in silence, gazing out to the horizon, he was tempted to ask her what was at the bottom of all this. But somehow, he dare not. He had the distinct feeling that it would make something explode and destroy her. It was obvious she had been hurt, but how? Could she have read the press in the last two weeks, in spite of what she said? And yet there hadn't been much about it really, the small column could easily have been overlooked.

John watched her dreamy face, the clear honey coloured skin with the peach bloom, he could never get out of his memory. That windblown fair wavy hair, that she wore a lot longer these days. The determined little chin. No, she was not capable of that sort of duplicity. She'd have faced him squarely with it.

None of this made sense to him.

Then unexpectedly, at last they shared a completely happy day. After lunch, they had driven out to the Lizard Lighthouse, and then set off on a long walk right across the grass tops of the cliffs, to Kynance Cove. A good stiff breeze had whipped the sea into curling waves with feathering wakes, which dazzled in the sun. Marion was happy, lifting her face into the wind, and swinging his hand as they walked briskly along the cliff top path. They stopped now and again, to watch big liners through his field glasses, as they steamed out into the Atlantic. She was free in mind at last, her expression and her mood were all tenderness — the Marion he knew.

The reached Kynance Cove as the tide was swirling in. The walk had been a bit long for Dinah, so John carried her under his arm. As they looked down from the top, he said, "I think this is the loveliest cove of all."

"So do I. It's quite unspoilt. Thank goodness there are no proper roads to it yet."

"Let's drop down and have a Cornish cream tea in the shack. Do you remember how your father enjoyed his cream teas there?" said John.

"I do. Wouldn't he be happy to know we are here like this... remembering him."

"Perhaps he does know."

And they did, all the time, while they ate through vast helpings of Cornish cream and strawberry jam, on home-made scones, as he was ribbing her about watching her weight, as she was chattering on happily.

After tea, they climbed the cliffside path, for the return walk to the Lizard. When she got a bit tired, he put his arm round her, to help her up the hill. She clung to it, and to his joy there was no need to withdraw it, this time.

They had only another half mile to go, when they sat and rested on the cliff top, and watched the rolling waves crashing on to the cliffs below. She suddenly lifted her face and kissed him of her own accord. He held her close and kissed her properly — the first time she had allowed him to do so, since he'd arrived.

When he lifted his head, he said, "when can we get married, my darling. We've waited so long." That was his mistake, but that thought was all that had buoyed him along.

She withdrew. Her face became an icy mask again.

"When?" John persisted urgently. He couldn't let her go on like this any longer.

"We can't! We never can. There's Amanda between us," she said wearily.

"But there isn't. Not any longer."

"What do you mean?"

"She's dead!"

Marion's went completely ashen. "John... how do you know?"

"She was found drowned in the Beech Farm well, at the end of the drive."

"When?"

"Two weeks ago."

"How... was she found?"

"By some workmen. The young couple you sold the house to, the Fletchers, were having Beech Farm put on to main drainage. The workmen were digging a channel for it, right across the line of the well. It was a deep channel. They sliced across the well and saw her body down it. So did Kate Fletcher."

Marion said nothing.

John went on: "She was identified by the jewellery she was wearing, and by her teeth fillings." He cleared his throat, distress made his voice do odd things. "There was a short column about it in in the press, though our local Western Echo reported it in fuller detail. But you must have missed it, while you were here."

"Did they find out... how long she'd be there?"

"About four months, they said. Must have just happened before you sold the house. If the Fletchers hadn't had the main drainage put in, her body would never have been discovered. That was a chance of fate, wasn't it."

"How have the Fletcher has taken it?"

"He's taken it pretty well, but it's upset Kate a lot. I just felt it was a good thing if it was to be discovered, that it happened after you'd sold the house. You might otherwise have had the place empty on your hands, for years afterwards."

"Why didn't you tell me about this before?" asked Marion.

"I badly wanted to, but your doctor had prescribed peace and rest for you. It's better for you that I shouldn't encroach on it, with my own problems."

"Treating me as if I was a half-witted child!"

"Not at all, my sweet. You need looking after. You've been recuperating after an illness. It must have been quite an illness, for the doctor to order such treatment, and for so long. You've lost a lot of weight, too."

"How... do they... think it... happened?"

John turned away. "The police have got it in hand," he said lightly to her.

"Yes, but... there must have been an inquest... and a verdict?"

"There was. The verdict was 'Murder by Persons Unknown'. The enquiry goes on."

"Oh God!" she said chokingly.

"The irony of it is, they suspect me at the moment. That's the reason why I came away. All that questioning, and snooping around the place, creased me."

"You a suspect? Why you, of all people?"

"It's my own fault, I suppose. You see, we had that time together at the summerhouse in Beech Farm copse, the night before you sold the house. I've never been so happy with you, and I think that went for you too. Next morning, I had to get down to the business at the estate farm, but all the time you were dominated my whole world. I hardly heard the problems that Harris my farm manager, was putting before me. After about an hour of this, I gave up. I just had to see you once more, before you left Beech Farm for always — even though we'd already said goodbye, earlier on."

"You... came to Beech Farm... that morning?" This sounded like a cry of alarm, from Marion.

John's eyebrows rose. "Yes," he said. "I left the farm office soon after 10 o'clock, collected Rufus my dog, and walked to Beech Farm copse, my usual route along the lane. But I never thought then to look in the cart shed first, to see if your car was still there, as it never occurred to me, that you'd already left. I knew your appointment in Salisbury at the solicitors, wasn't until midday."

"And I'd gone by the time you got there?"

"Yes, to my disappointment. It was such a drop, to find you'd gone, and were already out of reach. I looked all round for you, and when there was no sign of you, there was nothing left, but to make my way back home. And by the way, you'd left coffee in the percolator on the oil cooker. It was still boiling, it was lucky I was there to turn it out. Could have sent the whole hut up in flames, if it had been left."

"So, why does this make the police suspect you?"

"Because I was seen by Cowper, the new chap from the pub, pushing through the hedge into the lane. He was going for his morning ride," said John acidly.

"And?"

My presence on Beech Farm property, was thus confirmed, about the time they reckon that the murder took place. So beside you, sits suspect number one."

"But surely, didn't you tell them why you were there?"

"No."

"Did they ask you?"

"The whole blasted force seems to have asked me," said John bitterly.

"And you would never explained?"

"No."

"Why ever not?" she asked.

"It's not their business, its ours. I'm not having them poking their sniffling noses into our love. There are some things in a man's life that must not be touched."

"Oh John! You've got to get down to earth. Anyway, Chris Mainwaring will help you."

"No, he won't. I've seen him. He's become a policeman on the job, too. I've even had to send him my address while I'm away, in case I'm needed. Presumably to 'help police with their inquiries.'" He gave a dry laugh. She remained silent.

John turned to her. "But all of this is relatively unimportant. It'll fizzle out. They can't pin anything on me, it's just mere suspicion. I'm quite safe, as they can't prove a thing. But the main thing is, my sweet, that all this separation can come to an end. We can even get married now."

"But don't you think the police haven't thought of that? D'you think they are not at this moment, making out a case against you, based on their strong suspicion?"

"But they don't know about you and me. Nobody does."

"Somebody does!" She drew away from his arm and sat stiffly erect. "It's no good fooling ourselves, John. We can't marry, ever. She's still between us," said Marion, unhappily.

"That's ridiculous! In a little while, we'll be in the clear. When it's over, we can get on with our lives, hopefully together. Anyway, they can't convict a suspect, without proof."

"Can't they? You look back at criminal records, at the wrongly convicted cases. Some have even been hanged, when the death penalty existed."

"I think you're exaggerating, being a bit silly, my dearest."

Marion shook her head. "We'll never be in the clear. She is more between us now, dead, ever than she was when alive.," and suddenly Marion was shuddering with deep silent sobs.

He stroked the back of her bowed head and neck, over the softness of her hair. She flinched, as if he had stung her. He withdrew his hand.

His said through tight lips, "it's because you been ill that you feel like this." He sat stiffly, apart from her.

Dinah was whimpering, clambering up to her chest, and trying to lick her hidden face. Marion blindly put an arm round Dinah and buried her eyes in the warm furry neck.

It was extraordinary how Marion suddenly mastered her tears. She looked at John and gave him a bleak smile. She must have seen the anxiety on his own face. Her smile wavered on, as she seemed to draw on some hidden reserves of strength. She even took the initiative, now.

"Come on John, we'll walk on. I'll be all right now. Don't let's talk about it, any more. Let's be happy for the moment, and not allow Amanda to spoil even this." John was surprised, and disturbed, at the viciousness in her tone, in her last words. It was so unlike her.

She slipped her arm through his, and they walked back to the car. He wondered miserably, could she suspect him, too?"

*   *   *   *   *

All that evening there was a marked change in Marion. She was calm, full of self-assurance now, as if she had just driven out of a fog. He found she had ordered champagne for dinner, it was cooling in the ice bucket by their table. She let all the barriers down. Her love underlined every word of happiness, as she swept him along with her.

That night, he astonished himself, at the strength of his love. Her response was so wild, she was like a different girl. They had both become different people, almost like the desperation of sharing love for the last time.

Afterwards, he drifted into a deep sleep, and dreamt he was lying on the golden sands of a wide beach, with the tide run out. Wet seaweed hung from the rocks, and above him gulls were wheeling, crying to the waves.

22. Everything becomes clear, in the end

The next day, John and Marion, in their happiness, didn't want to look behind, or beyond that moment. They spent all afternoon with an old fisherman, and the catch had been good, even by his reckoning.

They wandered back to the hotel, along the path from the village which borders the shore, and then ascended the cliff through the bracken. It was here that there was a view of the sea on three sides. On the fourth side behind them, ran a narrow private lane, that joined the hotel to the main road. Near the top, they sat in the bracken for a while, to get their breath back.

Unexpectedly, Marion asked, "John, how did the two Fletchers react to all this, down their well?"

"It's been tricky. The cause of a lot of trouble to their marriage, it's driven a wedge between them."

"But why between them?"

"Well, as soon as they saw Beech Farm, they fell for it in a big way. But Kate Fletcher did so in a different way. She seemed to give the house an identity, almost as if it became a person related to herself."

"Isn't that strange," said Marion. "You see, that happened to me too. The house would be so happy."

He laughed. "You're as cuckoo over it, as she was! She isn't any more though. She wants David to sell up, and for them to go. She is unhappy with the house, feels it's let her down. She just wants to walk out on it, and leave it to its own problems."

"And David?"

"That's the wedge. He can't bear to go. Also, he's sunk a lot of money into it, all he's got. They were going to do the interior work themselves, but now she won't even lift a paintbrush."

"Oh dear. How do you know all this, John?"

"Well," said John, "he came around the other day, to look at some plans I have, for the archaeological dig at Upper Hinton. I noticed he seemed rather bothered and nervous — so unlike him. After a while, I asked him what was biting him, and he told me all about it. It seemed a relief to him, to be able to talk about it to another man."

"Poor them. I'm sorry."

"Oh, it'll be all right in the end, I know. I gave him some very sound advice, which he is taking."

"Really?" asked Marion. "And what might that be?" The old teasing note had crept into her voice again.

"I suggested he get her started with a baby as soon as possible. That is a sure cure for anyone with this imaginative sort of nonsense."

"You did, did you?"

"Yes," said John. "It's the obvious solution. Especially as it appears that she wanted to start a family, probably next spring, when the interior work on their house is finished. He told me he'd put a damper on it. He didn't want babies just yet. He wanted them to get used to living together in the country. She's very young, and he felt there was plenty of time before embarking on that as well. She was disappointed at the time, but let him have his way. But she told him, she wanted to put down their roots, in Beech Farm."

"So?" said Marion.

"I told him to get cracking. She'd be so thrilled, with her mind so full of it, and planning for the future, she'd forget all this nonsense about the house letting her down."

"How would he explain his sudden change of heart, to her?" asked Marion.

"We thought of that one, too," said John. "He'll say that her idea of starting a baby had been rolling around in his mind ever since she suggested it. The more he thought about it, the more it appealed. Only, why wait till next spring? Why not start now, straightaway? He felt sure he could handle that one, you see that is what she really wants above all else. So, it all seems solved. I hope to hear of Fletcher Junior being on the way, in 2 or 3 months' time. I'll even be happy to be godfather — after the helpful advice that I've given!"

"John darling. That sounds really funny, coming from you!"

"Why?" asked John. "It's what I would dearly love, myself. Marion..."

Marion interrupted quickly. "There are so many gulls now, since these oil slicks have been around. I always associate this place with cries of gulls. Look at them John! They're flowing off the headland and riding the empty sea troughs." She added, "the sea looks almost lilac, in this light."

But John wasn't listening. For some unaccountable reason, he kept looking back to the narrow private lane behind them. It became a focal point, he couldn't keep his eyes off it. He was not in the least surprised when finally, he saw a black car appear over the rise. Somehow he'd known it would come.

Without a word, he stood up. Marion was still dreaming over the gulls and didn't seem to notice. Two men in the black car saw him, as they got out of the car. They walked a few yards along the path and stopped in front of him. John swallowed, and could feel his heart pounding. Marion saw them, and abruptly stood up beside him.

John said quietly, "these men are Detective Inspector Williams and Detective Sergeant Turner, who are in charge of the investigation into Amanda's death." He turned to her, and saw an answer that seemed to rise to her lips, and then be stifled. She was standing beside him rigid, perhaps with terror.

Williams said firmly, "John Henry Gresham, you are charged with the murder of Amanda Gresham. I must caution you, you are not obliged to say anything unless you wish to do so, but whatever you say will be taken down, and may be given in evidence."

Before John could reply, he heard an icy voice from Marion, beside him. "Of all the stupid things, that's it. It holds about as much water as a butterfly net."

"I must ask you..." Williams began.

Marion interrupted. "You've got hold of the wrong person. I killed Amanda Gresham."

Williams and Turner exchange glances that showed no surprise. John wheeled round to her. "Marion, for God's sake be careful what you say! This isn't a joke, this is deadly serious."

"So am I, John," she said coolly. Terror had slid from her body. She had taken command of these three men, and the whole situation. "It'd be more comfortable if we all sat down, while I tell you about it. It's quite a long story." Her tone was as polite as a parson's wife, greeting a new member of the congregation.

The two detectives sat in the bracken, and she sat beside John. The way she slipped her hand into his was the only indication of her needing any support, outside her own strength. John turned to her, and said through clenched teeth, "Marion, I beg of you, think what you're doing!"

Marion no notice, and spoke to the two detectives. "I want you to listen carefully, as two human beings, rather than as policemen. My name is Marion Ferguson. I was the original owner of Beech Farm, after my father's death. John and I love one another, we have done so for nearly 5 years, now. But he could never have had a divorce and remarry as other people do, because of Amanda's mental illness. It made her entirely dependent on John, to look after her. He had to be there, when her spasms hit her. That was the trouble, you understand?"

Williams nodded, as he examined the horizon in silence. Turner concentrated on his shiny black toecaps in the bracken.

"So, we had to live our lives apart, as best we could. We used the summerhouse in Beech Farm copse for our rendezvous. I'm sure you will have thoroughly investigated that summerhouse."

Williams cleared his throat. "We have," he said.

"I don't know what we'd have done without it," Marion went on. "We met there as often as we could, some weeks it was almost every day. We bought all our thoughts, and ideas, and our lives there, to each other. In between was a sort of stored up silent diary, until we met again in the summer house. It kept us going. And no one knew then, did they John."

He couldn't speak. He could only cling to her hand, with both of his.

"And then my father died. I tried to live on alone at Beech Farm, because of John. But, because of John, I couldn't. It was all different after Father died. I found myself getting resentful and worked up, over every hour that he had to spend on Amanda, instead of me. I had accepted things as inevitable before, but now I became jealous of her, sharing even the little details of domestic life with him. It was a frustration that I could not bear. Why should she be allowed to sit opposite him by the fire, and at the dining table? I was on edge all the time, ready to blame him if he was five minutes late, cry with anger and jealousy — yes, jealousy — when he had to leave me. So now, instead of our relationship bringing peace and joy to us as before, it brought nothing but pain. So, one day, I took a long hard look at the situation — and knew it couldn't go on. I was spoiling the wonder that we had."

Her face softened at the memory. She held John's hand to her cheek. Turner fidgeted his feet on the bracken. Williams' eyes never left the horizon.

"So, I made the decision," Marion went on. "I put Beech Farm up for sale, on the market. I took an apartment in Salisbury, where I had a teaching job. I took it temporarily, until I formed a plan. Later, I took a job in Nottingham and lived up there — that is two years ago and now. Beech Farm remained empty until last April, and I couldn't bear to go near it, in that time. You see, I had loved the place."

The two detectives nodded their understanding.

"In those two years," Marion went on, "I struggled hard to break right away from the past, and most particularly, from my love for you, John. I couldn't tell you at the time, I'd have weakened too easily. I thought it was the easier way to fizzle it out gradually. That's why John, you only got sketchy notes from me, in answer to your letters. And I only sent these to keep my own sanity — at the time when I felt I couldn't go through with this." She was talking to him, oblivious of the presence of the two detectives.

"So that was it..." he breathed.

"And then, at the end of March, the estate agents wrote saying that they now had a firm offer for Beech Farm, from a young Salisbury architect, who had capital of his own to put down. The date for signing was April the 15th. And then I panicked. Beech Farm had been my life, and with John, and it would be lost to me — mine no longer. I made myself be sensible, but I also made a compromise. I wanted to be there in the summerhouse once more with you, John, before you, and all of it, passed out of my life."

John slipped his arm round her shoulders and drew her nearer to him. He too, was oblivious of Williams and Turner.

She said, "it's all right, darling. It's a relief to be able to tell it all to you now. So that's when I phoned you in London and asked to come down to the summerhouse to me, for the night of April the 14th, before I signed away Beach Farm at the solicitor's office next morning. Do you remember?"

"I remember all of it," John said in a deep voice.

"So that's why you returned unexpectedly to Larmer from London?" Williams asked, coming out of a trance.

"Yes," said John.

"That time together, made up for everything that had gone before," Marion said softly. "I think I never knew until then, the tremendous depth of your love. Next morning, when you left as the sun rose, I just didn't care what the rest of life had to offer. I had known the best. It'll stay with me always. I lay in bed for ages, re-living all of it. I got up soon after nine, dressed, packed my things in the overnight bag, and took it and Dinah along to the car. Then I came back and tidied up the summerhouse. There was a horrible finality over that tidying. I put the coffee on, and had some breakfast. The sun was pouring in from the clearing in front. I sat in the sun, and drank the coffee. I'd left the coffee percolator on the cooker, keeping it warm for a second cup. I had plenty of time, I wasn't due at the solicitor's office until midday."

"You said so, that night," said John. "That's why I couldn't understand, why you weren't there, when I went back next morning, for a final look at you."

"You'll see now," Marion said, with such a hollow sadness in her voice. "I sat in the sun, had decided to pick a bunch of daffodils, to take back to Nottingham with me — a sentimental last bit of Beech Farm. They were a glorious sight, and grew in great profusion, Inspector."

Williams nodded, still scanning the horizon. A seagull floated by, slow and silent as a ghost.

Marion drew in her breath sharply, and carried on. "Just as I started to pick them, Amanda suddenly appeared in Beech Farm copse. She flew at me, lashing out at me with her riding whip. Her face was wild and crazed. Her eyes seemed to have flames in them. I've never seen them before like that. I was terrified. So terrified, I couldn't move. Then she grabbed me, started beating me. The whip cut across my hand, my neck, my back — I couldn't escape that whip, it seemed to be everywhere."

John dropped his face into his hands, cowering as if the pain was cutting across him too. His heart was hammering. He held his breath behind clenched teeth.

"And then I'd twisted loose, and ran away as fast as I could. Away from stinging cuts of that lash. I ran and ran. Down the garden, past the house, down the drive. Anywhere to get out of reach of their terrible, flailing whip lash. I ran out of its reach, but in the drive I could hear her gaining on me, could hear her panting breath getting closer. Then the drive gate was shut, and that did it. She caught me, snatched at my arm, she had terrible strength, and I couldn't get away. She slashed and slashed at me with the whip — there was no dodging it. I tried to twist free, but she was too strong. I couldn't get away. I thought she'd kill me. I was twisting round and round, I couldn't see, with all the blood running into my eyes. The next thing I knew, she'd let go of me with a terrible scream, and disappeared. I wiped the blood from my eyes, and saw it was through the well doors."

For a moment Marion couldn't go on. There was utter silence, except for the crying of the gulls, and the waves slapping onto the rocks below. Then she continued in the low voice, "I went and looked down through the hole smashed through the well doors, but saw nothing. I remember calling to her, but there was absolute silence — not even a splashing, or the slightest ripple of water, just silence. She must have knocked herself out on something as she went down. I couldn't think then — I lost my nerve — got in a terrible panic. I could only think of running away, and not being found out. I looked at the broken well doors. A sheet of corrugated iron was on the leaf mould pit nearby, with leaves partly over it. It all looked otherwise undisturbed, and peaceful again. Then I walked back to the summerhouse, in a calm orderly way. I went from there straight to the car, and drove into Salisbury. I went to the roundabout route, over the tops of the Downs, so that I wouldn't have to drive through the village, and risk being seen." She was exhausted, by re-living all this.

"Then what did you do?" Williams' voice jerked her back to it.

"I went to a hotel, and straight along to the cloakroom. I washed the cuts with cold water, but they were deep and still bleeding a lot. I tied a handkerchief round my neck, and went to a chemist, and bought dressings, cotton wool, and bandages. I also bought two silk scarves, at the shop next door to it. I went back to the hotel cloakroom, mopped away the fresh blood, wrapped my neck in the dressings and bandages, and then wound a silk scarf over them, to hide them. Then I tidied myself, and removed the rest of the traces of the scuffle. I tied the other headscarf round my head, to hide the cuts in my ears. I still have the scars across the back of my neck, there is still very tender when they're touched."

"So that's why you shrank away from me yesterday," said John.

"Yes John. I couldn't explain why either, then. That is why I wear my hair long now, to hide the scars."

"Perhaps you'd allow us to look at your scars, if we may?" Williams asked.

Without a word, Marion lifted her hair. Even the seasoned detectives could be heard sucking in their breath. The lobe of her right ear was split into jagged strips. The back of her neck was quilted with healed purple weal's. One deep dark-blue scar ran across the back of the base of her skull, for one ear to the other. Williams thought that such a slash could have done serious damage. John could not bring himself to look at these scars. But the two detectives could see the truth of her description of the attack, from these scars.

"What did you do next?" Williams asked her softly, as she dropped her hair again.

"I rested in the hotel lounge, and drank several cups of coffee. Funny now, to think how I could have done all this so mechanically, after all that had happened. I got to the solicitor's office at midday, met the Fletchers, signed the papers, and then drove towards Nottingham. And then the rot set in. When I found I couldn't stop shaking, I put up at a hotel on the way, for a couple of days rest."

"Did you get your injuries treated at hospital, at all?" asked Turner.

"No. I wanted to, but I daren't. They'd have been bound to ask for some explanation — I couldn't risk that. I had to let nature heal them all, by itself. I imagine that's why my ear has healed in splits, as it should have been stitched. Luckily, I'm a healthy person, with good healing flesh, and nature did the job. But I'm still deaf in my right ear."

John cleared his throat, and dredged up his voice. "Darling, why didn't you tell me all this? Why? How could you carry all that alone? Surely, I was the one to tell?"

"I wish I had now," said Marion. "It would have saved a lot of pain for both of us. But I was terrified that if you knew I had killed her, it would change your feeling for me. You've loved her once and now you looked after her, as a crippled child. Your love for me was everything — it kept me going. I couldn't risk losing that."

Williams said: "If I may interrupt for a moment, Miss Ferguson, you didn't kill her. She died as a result of an accident."

"You mean..." Marion stuttered, "I'm not responsible for her death?"

"No, you're not."

"But I didn't even report it to the police. I ran away."

"There is no law that you have the report an accident that you've seen," said Williams.

"You have to report if you run over a dog in your car," said Marion.

"Yes, because you yourself have actually killed the dog. This was different. You didn't kill anyone in this case. She died by an accident."

"I felt I'd killed her. I've spent the last few months rubbing out the thought of you, John, and of Larmer, and anything to do with that life."

"So that's why you've never answered my letters," said John. "That's what your struggle, your illness, and your need for rest here in Coverack, has been all about." Now that the danger was over, John found sweat on his face.

"Yes, John. That's why. After all, I managed in Nottingham quite well for a bit, then I started having nightmares every time I went to sleep. I got so that I daren't sleep. It led to a bit of a breakdown. That's why the doctor advised me to go away, so I came here."

"Why didn't you come forward when you learnt about the discovery of the body, from the newspapers? You've had a few weeks to think it over," Williams asked.

"I never read about it," replied Marion.

John added: "She was under doctor's orders to have complete rest, no papers, just let the world go by, and lose count of time and days."

"So, when did you first know about it?" asked Williams.

John answered for her. "Yesterday afternoon, when I asked her to marry me."

"John," said Marion, "it was after that, that I decided to come forward and tell everything to the police. But not until our holiday together here was over. I wanted to have this time with you here first — and to face the music after that."

"Oh darling. That explains the change in you, yesterday evening."

Williams asked: "How did you know she was down here, Mr Gresham, if she had cut away for you completely?"

"I didn't," said John. "It was a total surprise to us both. I came here, back to the place where I have known great happiness, when Marion, her father and I, had all three stayed here together. I needed a rest too, with some reflected happiness, if only from the past."

"I'd already been here for a month, before John arrived," Marion explained.

"I see. Did you ever know what happened to the riding whip?" Williams asked.

"I never thought about that. I suppose it went down well with her."

"No, it didn't. Jimmy found it lying on the ground by the well, soon after she'd fallen in. He put the corrugated iron over the well doors," said Williams. "He picked up the whip and hid it under his mattress, it was his most treasured possession."

"But what ever made you think that John had murdered her?" asked Marion.

The two detectives exchanged a glance. "You might as well know our end of it, now that all the pieces have fitted together. Mr Gresham, by his contradictory statements, suspicious movements and behaviour, made himself a strong suspect, but we had no evidence. We knew that the speechless Jimmy was the key witness. So finally, we questioned him in the rectory, using Canon Pendleton as interpreter."

"Oh, the poor old Canon. It must have nearly killed him," Marion said.

"Yes, it wasn't very pleasant for him," Williams said. "But it had to be done in the pursuit of justice. Anyway, it transpired that Jimmy has been watching, and had seen you both. He went up to the Manor and refused to leave, until he'd seen Mrs Gresham, and told her. He thought he'd get a few extra apples, or sweets, for his trouble."

"He was always snooping round the woods and lanes," said John, tellingly.

"After he'd told Mrs Gresham, she set off for Beech Farm with her riding whip. You know the rest."

"Not quite," said Marion. "You haven't explained, Inspector, if Jimmy witnessed the whole thing, why did you charge John with her murder, just now?"

For the first time, Williams looked embarrassed. "We have to ferret out the truth, Miss Ferguson. Sometimes we have to use roundabout methods, to get to it. I gambled on charging Mr Gresham in front of you, that it would provoke you into giving us a confession... which it did."

"And how did you know I was here?" asked Marion.

"After seeing Jimmy, we went to Nottingham. When I found you were away, the lady in the apartment below yours told us where you'd gone. The moment we saw it was the same as Mr Gresham's forwarding address, it made everything much easier."

"How nice for you," said John acidly.

"What happens now Inspector?" asked Marion. "What I've told you is the absolute truth."

"I'm sure it is. Your scars bear ample witness to that," said Williams. "First, we must refer the whole thing to the Director of Public Prosecutions. You must write out a statement of all you've told us and sign it. We will forward this to the Director and await his decision. If he thinks a crime is involved, and you should be prosecuted, then you will be charged, and tried in Court. But if he thinks it was an accident, while you were running away in self-defence, then you'll hear nothing more, from any of us."

"And how do you think he'll see it?" asked Marion.

"It's extremely unlikely that you'll hear any more, from any of us, Miss Ferguson." Williams stood up. "I'll say goodbye to you both, and good luck. It's only in case the signatures are required — things of that nature. Well, we'll be getting on our way back to Salisbury."

"One moment, Inspector," said John. "Would you know whether Mr Pendleton found anything missing in my late wife's jewellery?"

"Yes, he did," said Williams. "The diamond and emerald set had gone, and a diamond spray brooch. He's charging Arnold Braithwaite with the theft — he got careless, left fingerprints inside the safe."

"But I don't intend to prosecute him," said John. "I don't want the jewellery, I'd prefer any insurance, if it can be claimed. He was a friend of my wife."

"So I understand," said Williams. "In the dossier compiled against him, she was his principal partner. But the prosecution doesn't rest on your hands, as this is a police prosecution. Mr Pendleton is waiting until you return, to report the full details to you."

"One other thing," said John. "How's Mrs Fletcher? Have you seen her lately?"

"She's very well now," said Williams. "I saw her only a couple of days ago, up to the eyes in paint! She lost heart in it for a while, after the shock discovery in the well, but they're both working hard at decorating again. She looks very well, and I could hear her singing away with the radio, as she painted."

John looked at Marian, and grinned. Turner said, "good luck to you both," as he got into the car and they drove away. Williams and Turner drove in silence for a while, then Turner said, "all the same, Sir, we can't escape the fact that there was this affair going on, all the time, between those two."

"That's their business, Frank. This affair did not lead to murder, and that's our business," Williams said crisply.

*   *   *   *   *

Marion and John stood together, watching the car till it was out of sight. Suddenly, the strength seeped away from Marion, and she sagged down onto the bracken. John sat beside her, and she rested against him, limply watching the sea.

"It's all over darling, all over. We can rub it out," said John, but he got no reaction from her. After a while he said, "we could get married straight away. There's no Amanda between us." But she shook her head.

"I know. But it is too quick after they found her. The village would be shocked to their roots. You're their idol, and we're going to live there," Marion's voice was weak with weariness.

"All right, we'll bow to their conventions. We'll get married at Christmas, in Larmer Church, and the Canon will perform the ceremony. Will that do for them?"

Marion nodded, and smiled up at him, a smile of utter peace.

"And d'you know what?" added John. "We'll fill that old Manor House with our children. The Fletcher's first-born will be only a little older than our own. We must get that dammed lake filled in though, it could be dangerous for children..."

She laughed softly, a laugh of pure happiness.

The Author

Alethea Lawson (nee Green) was born in 1907 in Concordia, Argentina, where her father was an Anglican Minister in the South American Missionary Society. At the age of six or seven, she and her family returned to England. She grew up in Dorset, in the village of Tollard Royal, where her father was the Church of England Rector.

She trained as a physiotherapist in London but relocated to Nottingham after meeting her first husband, Patrick Henry, a GP. They married in 1933. Patrick sadly died in 1944, where after Alethea restarted her physiotherapy practice, which was very successful. She subsequently specialised in teaching relaxation classes to expectant mothers in antenatal clinics throughout Nottinghamshire. In 1947 she married Hardy Lawson, who had been a stockbroker and had a distinguished career in the British Army during the Second World War.

In her later life, Alethea and Hardy moved to Whatton, a village in Nottinghamshire, in 1975. After Hardy's death in 1977 Alethea continued to live there until her own death in 2001. She is survived by three children and seven grandchildren.

The Cover Illustrator

York based artist Nell's 25-year career has spanned many disciplines from ceramics, portrait painting, textile art and more recently printmaking. Her work is fuelled by a love of learning traditional craft skills, and by a relentless enthusiasm for experimenting with colour. Her block print collections, inspired by the English countryside, are hand printed using painstakingly hand carved blocks, using unique and often unusual colour schemes. She describes the printing process as "...extremely satisfying. I love to experiment with combinations of colours to see what atmosphere they create. Colour is full of surprises." The block prints commissioned for this novel were inspired by the Dorset landscape and mid-century travel poster design.

***

For more information about this book, its author and illustrator, please visit **Annwyn House** online: http://annwynhouse.weebly.com